Falling for Fallon

Masters of the Prairie Winds Club

Book Twelve

by Avery Gale

Chapter One

"I'T'S TOO FUCKING hot for this shit." Fallon Foster gave the flat tire on her junker car one last kick before surveying the desolate stretch of highway surrounding her. The jerky movement shifted the heavy backpack she'd shouldered off one side. Stumbling to maintain her balance, she cursed a blue streak when her hip slammed into the car's solid fender. "Son of a fat fairy, no wonder this thing guzzles gas like a Sherman Tank... it *is* a tank." Fallon rubbed the aching spot on her hip and grumbled, "Just what I need, another damned bruise."

Fallon pulled the front strands of her jet-black hair into a ponytail on top of her head, leaving the rest of the thick mass tumbling down her back as she looked down the road, sighing in frustration.

"This is what I get for taking a GPS shortcut. This whole trip has been a special form of cruel and unusual punishment. Who knew the penalty for terrible taste in men was so severe? The Universe needs to get a sense of humor."

She hadn't seen another vehicle for so long, she wondered if she'd missed a road-closed warning. Fallon had never lived in a place where there weren't cars and trucks surrounding her 24/7. Being all alone beside a highway was eerie.

"Might as well get a move on." Rolling her eyes, she

muttered under her breath, "Probably better stop talking to yourself, Fallon, before someone drops a net over you. Damn."

Lost in thought, Fallon didn't hear the roaring of an approaching vehicle until it was close... much too close. The newer model sports car swerved at the last moment, barely missing her. The speeding vehicle veered off the road, sending up a dust cloud so thick, Fallon stumbled back onto the road. There was no way she wanted to risk falling into the ditch. The grass was so tall, she couldn't see the ground. Just the thought of getting too close was terrifying. This might be her first visit to the Lone Star state, but she'd seen enough westerns to be leery of thick prairie grass.

They have snakes in Texas, right? I'm sure they have rattlesnakes. And there are probably other poisonous things slithering around in that mess.

Fallon made the mistake of telling her ex-boyfriend she didn't like the slithering creatures, and he'd made it his mission to turn her discomfort into full-blown terror. A month ago, she'd opened the door of her beloved sports car to find a snake curled up on the driver's seat. After slamming the door closed, with enough force to make the small car rock side to side, she'd sold it for pennies on the dollar and bought the tank currently sitting fifty yards behind her.

My first mistake was getting involved with my boss.

Her life started spiraling out of control the moment she met Hagen Brody. Fallon worked her ass off to become a licensed pharmacist. It had taken her a year longer than her peers, but Fallon was debt-free when she'd finally walked across the stage to accept her diploma. Hagen's family owned a chain of stores scattered across the northeast, and she'd been thrilled to land what seemed like a plum position. At first, Fallon had been flattered by his obsessive need to know where she was at any given moment, naively thinking it was sweet he appeared so concerned about her safety. By the time she recognized his controlling behavior for what it was, she was already caught up in a cycle of physiological abuse.

Fallon heard the engine and whine of tires on hot asphalt a split second before pain exploded in her left side, and her body flew into the air as her feet left the ground. She wondered how everything around her was moving in slow motion as darkness closed in around her.

"I HOPE THE club isn't too busy tonight. Kent said they have a new bartender starting and asked if we'd show her around. It sounds like she'll be working at the club until she gets her pharmacy license transferred from New York to Texas."

Silas cast his friend a questioning look, wondering how the Wests had come on the woman's radar. While the Wests were certainly public figures, pharmacists weren't ordinarily on their recruitment list.

"I know what you are thinking. I wondered as well. Kent said this girl is the third cousin twice removed from Lilly's hairdresser's neighbor."

"What the hell?" Silas had grown up in a hippy community, where bullshit and trash talk were more common than not, but nothing had prepared him for the nonsense Special Forces operatives spouted. There were times, it was almost impossible to separate fact and fiction. In the years he'd been a member of the Masters of the Prairie Winds

Club, Silas discovered the more outlandish the tale, the more likely it was factually accurate. The place had a remarkably diverse membership. Prairie Winds Club members were a damned interesting group, and he'd come to think of them as an eccentric extended family.

"He was kidding... mostly, or at least I think he was joking. Hell, with Kent, it's hard to tell, and Lilly is a wild card, so anything is possible."

Kent and Kyle West's mother, Lilly, kept her husbands and sons on their toes. Polyamorous relationships were nothing new to Silas—he'd learned at an early age, love didn't always fit society's definition of normal.

"Have you finished setting up Lilly's computer net-work?" Silas was curious about his friend's latest project at the elder Wests' household. Carson kept his fellow Doms entertained with his stories about setting up the small network Lilly requested. The project kept expanding in scope and cost, but Dean and Del West just laughed when Carson presented the most recent estimate. Lilly's hus-bands had shaken their heads and assured him the equipment was less expensive than heavy artillery and bail money.

Lilly West's love for explosives and large weapons was well known. Her most recent adventure involved working with off-duty military officers she'd befriended. The group had blown up a small rowboat anchored in a lake near one of the local military bases. As it turned out, the manne-quins in the boat were a little too life-like for the nearby group of drone enthusiasts who alerted the police. Lilly told Silas that Deputy Fife hadn't listened when she and her friends explained they'd already secured permission from the proper authorities.

"I'm telling you, Barney is alive and well. He lives in

the next county, and I hope Andy doesn't give him a bullet."

The major and two captains were released to the base's commanding officer, but the over-zealous deputy insisted Lilly be held until her bond hearing. Del and Dean showed up with cash and an attorney. The young woman serving as Lilly's legal counsel had only been with the prestigious firm a short time, but she was well known by everyone at Prairie Winds. Lindy Timish worked as a nanny for several club families and was considered under the protection of the men and women. The submissives admired her for standing up to the Doms when they tried to micromanage different facets of her life. The Dom's adored her fierce spirit, and they'd continued interfering in her life more than she knew, but not as much as they'd wanted.

Silas might have felt sorry for the young woman if he hadn't been impressed by the way she handled Cameron Barnes. Cam was considered one of the CIA's most valued assets. He thought of himself as retired—the agency saw the situation differently. Silas worked with Cam occasionally and respected his work ethic and instincts. The man's resources were second to none, and his network of contacts was so extensive, there wasn't a chance in hell the agency would ever let him go.

Looking at Carson, Silas chuckled. They'd both heard the story of Lilly's arrest from the spirited woman herself. Silas had been relieved the experience hadn't dampened her spirit.

"I'm sure Lindy's impassioned speech at Lilly's bond hearing was a proud moment for Cam and CeCe."

Carson laughed out loud at the understatement.

"Lindy is the only person I know who gains the upper hand with Cam. If I didn't know better, I'd swear the two are related."

"Chloe is going to give Cam a run for his money as well. After all, she's had a hell of a role model." Chloe Barnes was already testing the limits with her parents' patience. She and her brother were both academically gifted, and their polar opposite personalities made the Barnes household challenging.

"Aside from the new bartender's interesting six degrees of separation, what do you know about her?" Silas enjoyed playing at the club but wasn't interested in settling down with one woman unless they could find one they both wanted. He and Carson had discussed sharing a wife; their only challenge was finding one who appealed to them both. It wasn't easy to find a woman willing to meet the demands of two sexual dominants with different goals.

Carson wanted to settle down and start a family right away. They both were at a place in their careers where they didn't need to push as hard as they had for the past decade. Having more free time to devote to a wife would help their bride adjust to having two husbands, especially if it wasn't a lifestyle she'd already been introduced to. Silas was more open to spending a few years enjoying the freedom to travel.

"Kent didn't seem to know much about her other than she had bartending experience. Evidently, that's how she worked her way through college. He did mention she'd left her job at a large pharmacy suddenly, but he wasn't sure what prompted it." In Silas's experience, professionals rarely left jobs suddenly unless there was a problem. Shaking his head, Silas wondered why the hell he was so interested in a woman he'd never met.

"Watch out." Carson's shout of warning was a few precious seconds too late.

Silas was damned glad he'd already slowed down when an idiot using his small sports car like a rocket flew around them. The fool swerved off the shoulder of the pavement, kicking up enough dust to reduce their visibility to a few feet. Of course, he'd chosen today to take the back road to the club. The one damned day a year when the wind wasn't blowing, and they'd driven down a dirt road. Without a breeze to clear the air, the dust remained suspended forever, creating so many shadows, he hadn't seen the figure on the edge of the road until it was too late.

Silas Vernon had lived in Texas for years but still considered the small community in the Colorado Rockies where he'd grown up home—no matter how much it changed between his visits. The one thing about Texas he never understood was the drivers' penchant for speed. He wasn't sure if it was the long stretches of open highways or the relatively flat roads, but whatever the reason, everyone over the age of sixteen seemed hell-bent on racing full-out between points A and B.

"I think you only clipped him with the mirror but damned if he didn't rocket off the side of the road. Fuck, I hope he's okay." Carson's assumption they were dealing with a man seemed off the mark to Silas. He was certain he'd seen long hair, but hell, that didn't mean anything either.

They'd noticed a disabled car a couple of miles back, and when Silas said he wondered what happened to the woman who'd been driving, Carson had shaken his head and chuckled.

"If the female subs at the club hear you say they can't change a flat because they are women, you'll never hear the end of it. Not all men are mechanically inclined. Do you want to ride in a car after I changed one of the tires?"

His friend had a point.

Carson Scott was as talented as any tech entrepreneur on the planet, but his automotive skills were limited to fueling up and programming the electronics in the cab. Put the man in a boat in the swamp, and he'd get you anywhere you wanted to go. Carson often joked that he hadn't ridden in a car until he started school, and Silas wasn't sure it was far off.

After bringing the truck to an abrupt stop, the two men sprinted back to the petite figure lying crumpled in the grass. The closer he got, the more convinced Silas was the person lying unmoving in the grass was a woman. Long jet-black hair fanned out from a bruised face, and long lashes brushed over dark circles under her eyes, making him wonder when she'd last slept.

"Fucking hell, you ran over an angel." Carson knelt beside the woman, the awe in his voice echoing Silas's opinion.

He was confident she hadn't actually been run over, but she certainly was going to be sore as hell from the jolt of being clipped by the pickup's side mirror. Taking in her appearance, he noted bruising along her cheek that was obviously from a previous injury. The mark was still well defined, but it would likely be eclipsed by the emergence of more black-and-blue marks appearing over the next few days.

When her eyes fluttered open, Silas was convinced his heart skipped a few beats. The woman had the most beautiful eyes he'd ever seen. The shade of ice blue was so crystal clear and haunting, he swore she was looking directly into his soul.

"What's your name, sweetheart?" She blinked several times as if she were trying to bring his face into focus but didn't answer.

"Chef, can you tell us your name?" Carson asked the question as he brushed a pebble from her cheek with the back of his fingers. Silas was convinced the move was more about touching her than removing a small bit of gravel from her face.

"Yes... I mean... I'm not sure. Give me a minute. I should know the answer to your question, right? Wait. What did you ask me? Why am I in the grass? I don't think I like tall grass, but... well, I'm not sure why." When she tried to sit up, Silas and Carson each put a hand on her shoulder.

"Stay still for a minute until we know you don't have any other injuries." Silas trained as an emergency medical first responder several years earlier when he started doing security work. He hadn't used the skills for a while but felt confident he'd recognize broken bones. It was obvious she was suffering from a mild concussion, but her pupils were the same size and reacting normally, so he wasn't concerned she was in any immediate danger.

"The driver of that blasted sports car should be strung up by his testicles. He scared the crap out of me, then swerved off the road and blasted me with dust and rocks... that's why I was in the road. Fallon... Fallon Foster. That's my name. You still wanted to know that, right?"

When she turned her face toward Silas exposing her bruised cheek to Carson, the smile faded from his face. Gone was the man who'd been enthralled a few seconds ago. In his place was the over-protective Dom, the unattached submissives at the club knew well.

The boy from the bayou whose mother died at his father's hand would step in front of a bullet to protect someone who couldn't stand up for themself. Carson had been away at college when his mother was killed, but Silas knew the images from the trial still haunted his friend. Forrester Scott had been an abusive bastard throughout his marriage, but Mary Lynn refused to leave the man she'd promised God she would love until death separated them—sadly, she'd kept her promise.

Chapter Two

CARSON KNEW FALLON Foster belonged to them the moment he and Silas knelt beside her on the side of the road. Her gaze connected with his, and the earth shifted on its axis. It felt as though he'd been looking for their "one" forever. It seemed sappy and cliché, but it was true, nonetheless. When he'd least expected it, she'd appeared... walking along the side of the fucking road. He'd lost his heart between one beat and the next... then he'd seen the fading bruise on her cheek and lost his damned mind.

"Who hurt you?" There must have been something in the tone of his voice that alerted the beauty at his feet to a dangerous shift in his demeanor. Fallon's pulse, so easy to see thundering at the base of her throat, kicked up several notches as she tried to scoot away from him. The quick movement made her groan as nerve endings numbed by adrenaline suddenly reawakened, and pain surged to the surface.

"We won't hurt you, sweetheart... well, not unless you ask nicely." Silas gave her what Tobi West called his panty-melting grin. Jen McCall referred to it as Silas's get out of jail free card after he'd seen her buying a pregnancy test in a nearby community and alerted Sam McCall. Sam immediately blabbed to his brother, and both her husbands were on her like superglue. When she'd confronted Silas, he'd flashed her an unrepentant smile that made Jen laugh despite her best effort to remain pissed.

Carson watched as Fallon's eyes widened briefly before she caught the underlying sexual innuendo. When she looked at the ground rather than answering his question, Carson shook his head in frustration. Damn it all to hell, he'd watched his mom make excuses for unexplained bruises and flat out deny their existence his entire life. After moving to college, Carson's visits became less frequent when he could no longer deal with his dad's abuse and his mom's denial.

"Who hurt you, Fallon?" Carson had no intention of letting her off without answering. He hadn't built a multi-million-dollar business by letting details slide.

"My ex-boyfriend. Note, I said ex… as in former." Either Fallon was feeling the effects of a head injury, or they were getting a glimpse of her personality in an unguarded moment. Carson considered sassy women a bonus—you had the intellectual challenge and the bonus of a sweet ass to paddle.

"So noted." Carson gave her a quick nod, letting her know he'd heard her, but it damned well didn't mean he was finished asking questions. He admitted to being a tenacious bastard but also understood the value of strategic timing. "Why were you walking, Chef? This isn't a well-traveled road. Catching a ride out here would be a crap-shoot at best."

"The odds of getting blasted with dirt are pretty impressive, and getting smacked by a monster mirror was a piece of cake." This time, when she tried to get to her feet, he and Silas helped her stand. Keeping their hands on her until she was steady meant they were close enough to hear her muttered, "And being rescued by two hot guys was easy-breezy." Silas looked at Carson, their gazes easily meeting over Fallon's head.

"Where were you headed, sweetheart?" It seemed Silas was going to play the good cop and let Carson play bad cop. They were roles the two of them easily traded back and forth, so it wasn't difficult for either to follow the other's lead.

"Have you ever heard of the Prairie Winds Club? I was supposed to report to work there…" Fallon looked at her bare wrist and sighed. "Damn, I keep forgetting I left my… ummm, I mean, I don't have a watch anymore. No matter, I'm sure I'm late. Crispy critters and alphabet soup, I hope I don't lose out on the position because of a flat tire."

"So, you're the new bartender?" Carson watched as she pulled her lower lip between her teeth, her brows drawing together as she nodded.

"I did some—well, actually *a lot* of bartending in college. It will take a while to straighten out some challenges with my pharmacy license. The stupid jackass I dated put the skids on my transfer."

The last was whispered so softly, Carson would have missed it if he hadn't been looking at her. His computer skills would make looking into her background easy enough, but Carson preferred she told them what they needed to know. No matter how justified the search, it would feel a lot like stalking unless he was convinced her safety was at stake.

The line between a Dom's care and a submissive's right to privacy was blurry at best and too often ignored for Carson's peace of mind. He'd made millions using technology to gain information people wanted to keep private, but that didn't mean he didn't understand the moral implica-

tions of using his skills to spy on a woman he was interested in.

"We'll be happy to give you a lift to Prairie Winds and
vouch for you about the flat, but I can assure you, the club
owners' only concern will be that you were on a seldom-
used road in a car they won't deem road-worthy. We were
already headed that way. Kent and Kyle asked us to show
the new bartender around the club."

Silas was a born flirt. He blamed his upbringing, but his
friends all insisted it was a personality trait. Carson had
seen Silas's charm turn on and off like a switch, so he was
convinced it was more a tool than a trait.

"Honestly, no one should ever trade my luck for talent.
I can't believe I have been busted by a couple of dominants
charged with giving me the grand tour of my new work-
place. Seriously, how do I *always* manage to stumble into
these things?"

Carson couldn't hold back his chuckle at her frustrated
muttering—if they paid close attention, he had a feeling he
and Silas would learn more from her self-talk than from a
regular conversation.

FALLON WOULD HAVE figured they were joking if she hadn't
recognized her usual battle with fate. Honestly, this was
exactly the sort of thing that should send up all sorts of
warning flags. She should call a repair service, get the tire
fixed, then get back on the road. Sure, she'd disappoint her
mom's friend, Lilly West. She'd only met the woman a few
times and liked her, but that didn't mean she should ignore
all the signs of impending disaster and stay.

"Chef, I'd suggest you push all those thoughts of running right out of your head."

"Disappointing Lilly West is never a good idea. Remember, we're talking about the woman who thinks blowing things up is great fun and should be an Olympic sport."

Silas gave her a conspiratorial wink, making her wonder if he was joking or serious about Lilly blowing up stuff. *Geez, Louise. You'd think that was a detail my mom would have mentioned.*

The romance novels that filled Fallon's e-reader focused on the dominant and submissive lifestyle. The men she'd dated were on two ends of the spectrum—those who were so meek, she hadn't even considered mentioning the things she'd wanted to try, or they were wannabe Doms, who mistook controlling for dominance. Fallon had a habit of putting herself in poor company. Poor decisions... one of the traits she'd inherited from her parents.

Carson grabbed her backpack as Silas led her to the pickup. It was easy to see the two were used to working together. Their movements appeared almost choreographed. She briefly wondered if they shared their women. She was going to have to rein in her curiosity about kink, at least until she was no longer working at Prairie Winds. Gawking at the clientele was the fastest way she knew to lose a job.

As a pharmacist, Fallon walked a fine line between interacting with customers, making certain they knew she was concerned with their health, asking questions to make sure they understood the instructions, and what side effects they might experience as opposed to asking questions they considered intrusive and judgmental.

Getting involved with her boss had been an epic mistake. During her cross-country trek, she'd turned the promises to herself to make better decisions into a mantra—repeating it over and over, hoping it took root. The realization she could well be on the cusp of making another rash decision, Fallon stopped. The move was so sudden, the men took a couple of steps before realizing she was no longer beside them.

"Fallon?" The man who'd introduced himself as Silas paused, his expression thoughtful as he turned to her.

She didn't know these men. Was she a fool for letting them lead her to their truck? There was something about them her heart trusted, but her head was screaming at her to remember the nightmare she'd just escaped. Fallon appreciated her strengths, but after the disaster with Hagen, she recognized her habit of trusting the wrong men. Silas and Carson exchanged a look she couldn't interpret, and it took every bit of her self-control to keep from taking a step back.

"Do you have Kent or Kyle's phone number, Fallon?" When she shook her head, Carson's expression darkened as his gaze flickered in Silas's direction. "We need to remind the Wests how important it is for them to share their contact information with new employees."

"I had it, but I ditched… umm… I recently changed phones and didn't take time to transfer all the information." More like she'd tossed her phone and smartwatch off a bridge when she remembered Hagen bought them. She'd known there was a good chance he was tracking her. This time, the look the men exchanged was easy to read— they knew she wasn't being completely honest with them, but they weren't going to call her on the deception… yet. She'd read enough to understand this was one of those "keep your snarky comments to yourself" moments.

Pulling his phone from his pocket, Silas held it out so

she could see the screen as he scrolled through his recent calls before highlighting Kent West's name. When Fallon realized Silas was using Facetime, she reached up to smooth her windblown hair, took a deep breath, and hoped she didn't look too worse for wear. The man who answered was younger than she'd expected. His smile appeared genuine, and she might have missed the brief look of surprise when he realized Silas wasn't alone if she hadn't been watching for it.

"Silas, want to tell me why I see our new bartender standing beside you on... holy shit, is that the river road?"

"It's a long story, and we'll be happy to give you all the details when we aren't about to melt. What we need is for you to reassure Fallon we are members of the club and can be trusted to deliver her safely to your door."

She saw a flair of approval in Kent West's eyes as he gave Silas a quick nod and turned his attention to her.

"Fallon, I know we haven't had the opportunity to meet in person, but we're looking forward to you joining our team. I'm happy to hear you asked for confirmation before getting into a vehicle with strangers. You will be safe with Silas and Carson. My brother and I asked the two of them to show you around the club this evening." His attention was drawn to someone she could hear speaking out of the camera's view. She didn't have to wait long to find out who'd joined him.

"Hello, Fallon, I'm Kyle West. Cam Barnes tells me there is a disabled car registered to you along the river road. We've dispatched a crew to bring it to the club. They will put your things in the apartment upstairs." She knew Kent and Kyle West were twins, but she was shocked by how much they looked and sounded the same.

"Wait... I thought I was staying in one of the small cabins by the river. I'm not sure I can afford the rent for a larger place." Kyle West frowned, making Fallon wonder if she'd already landed on her new boss's bad side.

"Fallon, I think there has been a misunderstanding. I don't know where you got the impression you'd be paying rent, but that's not how we do things around here. We have some concerns about your former employer." Fallon didn't miss Kyle's slight pause between the last two words, and from Carson's furrowed brow, he hadn't missed it either. "You'll stay in the apartment upstairs until we're convinced he isn't going to problem."

Hagen made a lot of threats when she refused to be forced into a sexual relationship with him—particularly one involving another woman. Maybe it was selfish, but she had no plans to share any man she was sleeping with. Sighing to herself, Fallon hated how hypocritical it made her sound to admit she'd fantasized about two men bringing her pleasure, but she couldn't help the way she felt.

Her ex-boyfriend's verbal thrashings and emotional manipulation had made her feel smothered. He'd badgered her about her parents, constantly inquiring about her inheritance. The final straw was the night he pushed her down the staircase because she'd refused to participate in a ménage with a young female clerk from the store where Fallon worked. Maybe it was selfish, but she had no plans to share—particularly not with a girl who'd only had her driver's license for a couple of years.

Fallon knew about the Wests' military backgrounds and their contract work for Uncle Sam since retiring as Navy SEALs, so she wasn't surprised when the alerts started hitting her phone, letting her know they were doing an extensive background check. Her dad had shown her how to set up alerts on the internet when she was in high school. He'd told her it was in her best interest to know when someone was making inquiries, and he'd been right. One of the things she wondered about on the drive to Texas was why Hagan hadn't checked her background before hiring her as a pharmacist. Now she was worried about the Wests' strange feeling she might be in danger despite the fact she'd moved across the country.

Damn it all to prickly pears, what do they know that I don't?

Chapter Three

SILAS STIFFENED WHEN he heard the underlying concern in Kyle's voice. The man was stone cold when it came to security concerns. Silas had never met team leaders who could analyze a situation as quickly and accurately as the owners of the Prairie Winds Club. Their team of contract operatives was recruited from the upper echelons of their respective fields. Kent and Kyle were protective of all their members and employees, but knowing they'd moved Fallon from one of the cabins into the ultra-secure apartment above the club spoke volumes.

"We'll be there in five minutes. I assume whoever you're sending won't need Fallon's keys?"

Silas heard Kent laugh from out of the camera's range at the same time Fallon asked, "Why wouldn't they need the keys?" Carson stepped forward, drawing Fallon's attention away from Silas's phone.

"Car locks won't stop anyone Kent or Kyle would send. To be honest, from the looks of your car, the locks probably wouldn't stop most third graders." Carson's observation probably wasn't too far off the mark, but Fallon didn't appear to appreciate his sarcasm.

"That was just rude. I know the car isn't anything special, but it got me here, and I didn't even use the whole case of oil the salesman threw in."

If Silas hadn't noticed the corners of her mouth turn up

a fraction of an inch, he would have believed she was really offended by Carson's remark. What he didn't know was whether or not she was kidding about the oil. If not, she would have a hard time convincing anyone at Prairie Winds the car was worth keeping.

"We'll see you soon." Kyle turned to his brother before disconnecting the call, his voice stern and dripping with sarcasm of his own. "What kind of moron has two first names?" The call disconnected as Fallon giggled.

"Probably should have been a clue. It makes him sound like a teeny bopper who uses his first and middle name on stage." Fallon shrugged before walking to the car. "It's hot. I hope this fancy truck has air conditioning. My body is going take a while to acclimate to these third level of hell in May temperatures."

"Sweetheart, if you think this is uncomfortable, July and August are going to be a rough ride." Silas let Carson lead Fallon to the passenger side as he slid behind the wheel and cranked up the air conditioning. He smiled when his friend helped her into the front, seating her between them rather than using the rear seat.

They were only two miles from the club, so they were passing through the large front gate within a couple of minutes. Fallon hadn't said anything during the short drive, but Silas could practically feel the nervous energy pulsing around her. Parking in one of the spaces reserved for the club's dungeon monitors, he was grateful they'd be able to walk Fallon along the shaded walk to the back entrance.

"Thank you for the ride. I'm sorry you had to turn your truck into a meat locker." Fallon tried to shift her knees to the door, but the movement was stifled by Carson's long legs. Silas wanted to laugh at the startled look on her pretty face when she realized he wasn't moving. The woman was an open book, her emotions playing out on her face clearly. She was uncomfortable with her attraction to them, and he understood how strange it must feel if she didn't have any experience with polyamorous relationships. He could also well imagine she wasn't looking to jump from the frying pan into the fire if her previous relationship ended poorly.

It might take her a few weeks, but once Fallon had an opportunity to spend time with Tobi and Lilly West, Gracie McDonald-Drake, and Jen McCall, she'd understand the benefits of having two men focused on your pleasure. Like the other men at the club, Silas and Carson worked long hours and traveled more often than they wanted to. Most of the time, it would be easy for them to juggle their schedules so their submissive would never be home alone. If they were lucky enough to find a woman willing to be their wife, they'd make certain it was a decision she never regretted.

"We'll show you to the apartment and make sure you're settled. If you want to take a shower, we'll make sure you have everything you need."

"Oh, no, I'll be fine. I'd appreciate some help with my bags if there isn't an elevator. I don't have too many, but they're pretty heavy. I'd win a gold medal if packing was an Olympic sport."

Silas grinned over her ducked head at her swift response when Carson mentioned showering. Despite her jet-black hair and slightly tanned complexion, Fallon's blush was a deep rose. Hell, Silas wasn't sure he could remember the last time a woman in his care blushed.

"Don't panic... yet, Chef. If you had let me finish, you'd know I was trying to tell you the shower in the apartment is a technological wonder. I've never met anyone who didn't need help figuring it out."

Carson's voice was calm but firm enough for Fallon to see there were rules she'd need to follow. Her employment at the club would offer her some leeway with the club's strict guidelines, but there were some points of protocol every submissive was subject to and interrupting was one thing none of the Doms would overlook.

"I'm sorry. I swear I'm not usually this jumpy or rude. It's just that... well, you two are a lot, and the last time I trusted someone on sight, it didn't work out well for me."

That was the second time the hair on the back of Silas's neck stood on end since he'd met Fallon. He understood the challenges between exes, but there was something more he hadn't been able to identify. There was an underlying air of fear and vulnerability surrounding this woman, something he wasn't sure she was even aware surrounded her. No doubt, the Wests would have many of the answers, and Cameron Barnes could fill in any blanks.

Silas had never met anyone as well connected as Barnes. For a man who claimed to be retired, he was still ass deep in alligators, as Carson was so fond of saying. Every time there was an incident involving the club or its members, Cam or Cooper was involved. Both men had worked for the CIA, and in Silas's experience, there was no such thing as a retired Agency operative. The sound of Fallon's quiet voice brought him back to the moment.

"It's hard to imagine a shower so complicated, some-one would need tech support. Are you certain I can't figure it out?"

"Positive. Let's go." Carson wasn't particularly patient on his best day and seeing the bruise on Fallon's cheek pushed him past any semblance of being civil. By the time they reached the door leading directly to the apartment's private elevator, Kent West was waiting for them.

"Damn, I thought maybe you changed your mind, Fallon. Did these two have to convince you my brother isn't an ogre to work for? I'm Kyle's good-looking and charming brother, Kent. Welcome to Prairie Winds."

Fallon extended her hand, and Silas stood back, watching as it was quickly engulfed by Kent's much larger one. Damn, her hand looked tiny in his monster mitt. It was all Silas could do to keep from growling at the sight of her hand in Kent's. By the time he looked up from their clasped hands, Kent was grinning like a damned Cheshire cat. Kyle West might be considered the boss at the club, but it was an illusion.

Hell, Silas had known businessmen and women who believed they were dealing exclusively with Kent or Kyle when, in fact, they'd been dealing with both. They played alternating roles of good cop/bad cop easier than any pair he'd ever worked with, although they seemed to switch less frequently the past few years. There were few people outside their team of contract operatives who knew how skilled the men were or how well-respected they'd been as team leaders in the SEALs.

When Uncle Sam found out they were retiring, their commanding officer suggested they start their own team. Kent once told him it was the best career move they'd ever made. They had more freedom with their missions, could refuse a job they deemed too dangerous, and contracting was more lucrative than they'd ever dreamed possible.

Silas understood the monetary aspect of working independently, but he had no interest in the kind of work the Prairie Winds team took on. He'd worked in law enforcement until a few years ago. Private security let him follow an entirely different set of rules and paid exponentially better. He'd always wondered why taxpayers refused to acknowledge the importance of people who taught their children and those who protected them. Wages for teachers and law enforcement would never be enough incentive. Anyone choosing one of those professions did so because they considered it a calling.

"I had a flat tire. It seems the slick salesman who sold me the car neglected to mention there wasn't a spare. If it's alright, I'd like to freshen up before I start my shift. I might have underestimated how hot it would be in Texas."

Silas grinned when Fallon tried to pull her sweat-soaked turtleneck sweater away from her skin. They'd have to make certain she had clothing more suited for Texas summers. If she thought it was hot now, she was in for a rude awakening.

"Take all the time you need. We didn't schedule you behind the bar tonight. Silas and Carson will show you around. It's important you have time to acclimate to the environment before being asked to mix drinks with so much going on all around you."

What Kent left unsaid was how closely she'd be monitored for any signs of discomfort, disdain, or judgmental behavior. Any of those would jeopardize her job, but Silas's gut instinct told him she was a natural submissive. It was a safe bet in her previous relationships, she'd been too intimidated to express her interest in the lifestyle. The more he watched her, the more curious he became. Who was her ex-boyfriend, and what the hell happened to send her across the country?

Silas signaled Carson, letting him know he planned to speak to Kent before joining them upstairs, then gave Fallon a quick kiss.

"I'll be right up, sweetheart. Do you need for me to send up someone from the first aid station?" Fallon looked confused for a few seconds before her cheeks flushed.

"No, but thank you for asking. My shoulder might be a bit stiff tomorrow, but I'll work it out."

"Carson will show you how to set the shower, so the jets massage your sore shoulder. It will help minimize any residual stiffness." Kent's smile and dancing eyes made him appear younger than Silas knew he was. As the doors of the elevator slid closed, Kent added, "I'd like to tell you that's why we installed the shower, but everybody and their three-legged dog knows better."

Silas and Kent both chuckled when Fallon's eyes went impossibly wide; Kent's meaning hadn't been lost on her.

Once the elevator began its ascent, Silas leaned against the frame of the closed door, giving Kent a searching look.

"Talk to me."

"I don't know as much as you might think. Remember, she is here because she's the daughter of one of my mom's oldest friends. I do know she took a big financial hit to move, so whatever happened between Fallon and Hagan Brody must have been significant."

When Kent looked like he was considering how much to reveal, Silas cleared his throat, letting the other man know he wasn't going to let it go.

"The guy has some interesting family connections. His grandfather was a skilled and well-respected chemist specializing in pharmaceuticals. Unfortunately, the lure of money was stronger than his moral compass. He fell in with criminals who make you wealthier than you ever imagined possible, but there is no end to their demands."

"And now? Does the family still have ties to organized crime?"

"Likely, though they've built a large enough fortune to hide it. The grandfather died a few months before Fallon's parents, leaving the business to his only son. Hagan's father is twice as mean and half as smart as his old man. Neither he nor Hagan passed the test to get their pharmacist license. The one area where they excel is recruiting."

"I assume this is the point where Fallon enters the picture?"

"It seems so, but we're waiting for Cam to get back from vacation to clear up some details." Kent ran his hand through his hair in frustration before continuing, "I hate it when CeCe drags his ass off to some damned remote island with no fucking internet. What the hell is with her wanting to be so isolated? If we tried to take Tobi to a place with no cell service, she'd skin us alive."

Silas couldn't hold back his laughter because anyone who knew Tobi West understood the truth of her husband's words. Tobi was one of those rare people who lived life to the fullest and damn the consequences. It was a good thing she had two husbands because Silas doubted there was any one man who'd be able to keep up with her. Her antics kept Kent and Kyle on their toes, and the club rumor mill kept her from hiding her activities. The damned grapevine kept Kent and Kyle supplied with enough fodder for the most hardline gossip.

"Who am I skinning alive?" Tobi stepped into the small vestibule and promptly received a solid swat on her barely covered ass. "Sorry, Sir. It always takes me a few minutes to get my head back into club mode. Please don't tell Master Kyle. He's already pis... unhappy with me."

"Valliant attempt, Kitten. Unfortunately, I don't think anyone was fooled." Kent and Silas chuckled when Kyle stepped from the shadows. Tobi winced when she realized he'd heard her comment. *Why on earth didn't the woman stop digging when she was already in the hole with one of her Doms?* "I'm sure Kent will be interested in hearing about our earlier encounter. Do you remember my warning that any additional infractions would result in a punishment?"

To her credit, Tobi didn't respond since Kyle hadn't asked a question. Kent turned to Silas and shook his head. The quirk of Kent West's lips told Silas he wasn't actually upset with his sweet wife. Tobi might be a handful, but the woman had a heart as big as her home state of Texas. Her loyalty to her family and friends was unquestioned, and she was a brilliant businesswoman.

Tobi and her best friend, Gracie, had spent several years building an amazing marketing plan for the implementation of retail boutiques into clubs all over the world. Their Forum Shops business model had become so successful, the two women were practically revered by the small business owners they'd taken along on their wild ride to the top of BDSM club clothing and equipment sales.

Gracie's husbands, Micah Drake and Jax McDonald, led the club's high-tech security team. From the control center, affectionately referred to as Mission Control, the men sitting in front of the panel of monitors could see every square inch of the club and surrounding acreage, save the toilet areas. The locker rooms were only displayed if there was an issue, but there had been enough of those for Kent and Kyle to decide to install monitoring equipment.

When the inevitable questions about privacy arose, Kent politely reminded the few who expressed concerns they'd signed away their presumption of privacy when they joined the club. Kyle was less tactful, explaining anyone walking around naked in full view of other club members, fucking as a spectator sport, or waving their wanker out in the open for a blow job, had no business bitching about privacy.

Kyle's blunt response had set off ripples around the room, and to no one's real surprise, it was Dean West who offered a compromise. Kent and Kyle's dad suggested they add a flashing light to indicate when the cameras in the locker room were active, but it was Tobi who'd truly broken the ice, jumping to her feet and wrapping her father-in-law in a huge hug before he could take his seat, exclaiming, "Isn't my pops brilliant?" Silas could swear the man blushed under his tanned face, lined with the marks of years of wisdom. Tobi's people skills were remarkable by any measure. Knowing the physical and emotional abuse she'd endured as a teen made her bubbly personality all the more remarkable.

"Yes, Sir, I'm sure he'll be thrilled." She'd let so much more hanging unspoken in the air between the three of them, Silas struggled to hold back his laughter.

"As much as I'd love to stick around and watch the show, I'm heading upstairs to check on Fallon. Leaving her alone too long with Carson is risky." Kent and Kyle both muttered terse agreements making Tobi giggle.

Professionally, Carson was the most thorough bastard on the planet, but when it came to D/s, he often pushed too hard, sending even the most experienced submissives scurrying in the other direction.

"We'll talk again tomorrow as scheduled." Silas already planned to meet with the Wests to let them know what they learned while escorting Fallon around the club. Suddenly, the stakes for that meeting were exponentially higher.

Chapter Four

S TEPPING INTO THE apartment atop the club, Fallon couldn't hold back her gasp. The place was stunning. During the short elevator ride, Carson told her the Wests had moved out after their children were born. Tobi hadn't wanted the kids raised in such a public setting, so their expansive apartment was used for visitors and new employees. Fallon looked around, amazed anyone would move out of such a beautiful home.

Carson gave her a quick tour of the open area of the apartment, pointing out the hall leading to the bedrooms and promising to show her the safe room before they went back downstairs. When she realized her luggage and boxes were already sitting on the dining room table, Fallon wondered aloud how anyone could have completed the task so quickly.

"You'll find those working for the Wests are remarkably efficient. Some of them are former members of various branches of the military, but the truth is, they only hire the best of the best. Getting your things up here quickly wouldn't pose any problem for them."

"That sounds a lot like a warning, Carson. I might not have tended bar for almost a year, but I think it will come back to me fairly quickly." She hadn't intended for her response to sound snarky, but damn it all to happy hell, she was tired and sweaty, and Carson looked like he'd just stepped off the pages of a fashion magazine. *What's with that? Don't Texans sweat?* When he raised a brow, clearly unimpressed with her tone, Fallon sighed. "I need a shower and a couple cups of strong coffee."

The damned man simply grinned as he leaned back against one of the side tables. With his ankles casually crossed in front of him, he watched her closely. A shiver shot up her spine before branching out like lightning, traveling all the way to the tips of her fingers and toes. What was it about this man that made her skin tingle with awareness? The feeling had been equally unsettling with Silas, adding to her confusion.

"You'll get your coffee. I'll call it in while you shower. Now strip."

Nothing about Carson's body language or tone indicated he was joking, but she was still shocked to her toes. What in heaven's name made him think she would strip in front of him? Fallon suddenly wondered if she'd fallen into another dimension.

"Fallon, I assure you, you do not have anything I haven't seen before. The laundry room is behind us, so there is no reason for you to traipse through the apartment in sweat-soaked clothing."

"We just met. I'm not in the habit of stripping in front of… well, in front of anyone, actually." Her mind was racing when for the first time, she considered she was well and truly in over her head. Sure, she'd always thought dominance and submission was something she wanted to explore, but now she felt as though she was floundering. To her great relief, Carson appeared completely unfazed by her reaction. Standing stock-still, he watched her with an intensity that made her feel as if he was trying to listen to her thoughts.

"One of the things you'll learn quickly working in the club is Doms don't like repeating orders. Even the most lenient dominants will put you over their knee for making them give you a command twice."

It took her mind several beats to process what he'd said, and she felt her face heat thinking about being draped over Carson or Silas's knee, with her ass peaked high as the first handprint bloomed pink on her bare skin. A soft chuckle from Silas startled her out of her mini-fantasy and back to the moment.

"I'm not sure that was much of a threat, Carson. As a matter of fact, I'd say Fallon looked lost in the pleasurable possibility."

Fuck a duck. How long had he been standing there? Obviously, one man was more than she could deal with, so how the hell would she ever survive being alone with two?

"She seems a bit dazed. If she isn't capable of taking off her clothes, I'd say we have two options—help or insist she seeks medical attention. It's always possible the spill she took into the ditch was more of a problem than she wants to admit."

Fallon might be struggling to keep up with everything taking place around her, but she wasn't so flustered, she didn't recognize first-class manipulation when she heard it. She wasn't as frustrated by the command to strip as she was at his blatant attempt to push her to comply. When she met his gaze, the challenge in his eyes was tempered by a look of desire, sending a wave of heat coursing through her entire body.

"I spoke to both Kent and Kyle downstairs, Fallon. I explained what happened and told them you'd assured us you were fine. Did I speak too soon?"

"I might have been an only child, but I had enough

friends with siblings to recognize a dare when I hear one."
Fallon knew she should have been annoyed by Silas's
challenge, but the glint of mischief in his eyes held a boyish
charm she couldn't resist. Grateful the Wests were going to
provide her fresh clothing for the evening, she grasped the
bottom hem of her sweat-soaked shirt and yanked it over
her head before tossing it in the direction of the laundry
room. "I don't know why you are so hell-bent on seeing
me naked. Bumps and jiggles aside, I'm no different from
any other woman." She bent over to untie her sneakers
when heat seared her right ass cheek, the crack of a palm
connecting with tight denim following quickly after. "Hey!
What the holy fuck a fairy was that for?"

"You are not to speak negatively about yourself. Words
have power, so use them wisely." Carson's glare kept her
from telling him exactly what she thought about his
highhanded behavior.

"What happened to *my body, my voice*?" She disliked the
sullen tone she heard in her voice but was too lost in the
rush of warmth between her thighs to do anything about it.
Damn, she hated knowing her body was betraying her.

"Part of our job is to make certain you are ready for
what you'll encounter downstairs. Let me tell you what I
see." Silas stepped forward, cutting the distance between
them in half. He wasn't so close she had to strain to meet
his gaze, but his shift in position sent a clear message.

Fallon had known she would meet Doms when she
applied for the bartending position at a kink club but hadn't
known how quickly her own limits would be tested. Sure,
she was interested in the sexual dynamics of a D/s relationship, and a ménage with two men who sent her pulse
racing certainly wouldn't be a hardship. Fallon's real
challenge was her own self-sabotaging habit of rebelling.

Even if it was something she wanted to do, the minute someone told her to do it—all bets were off.

"Do you see what I see, Silas?" Carson's voice broke through Fallon's mental debate.

She made a split-second decision to head off whatever Carson was planning to share. Damn it, she was hot and sweaty. She wanted the shower more than she wanted to hide from two men who had no doubt seen women with better bodies.

"I love women with spirit—the ones who will push back and demand we earn their submission."

Silas's words made her heart swell. Fallon wanted to learn more about the side of her personality she'd always felt the need to suppress… until now.

"Might as well lose the bra, Chef. That little bit of lace isn't hiding anything. Your rosy nipples are on full display. Those bits of flesh are peaked to perfection, and I can only hope whatever you plan to wear this evening gives us unfettered access."

Flipping open the front clasp of her lacy bra, Fallon let it slide down her arms before Carson's words registered.

"Wait. What? Isn't there some sort of uniform for bartenders? It was my understanding I would still be on the clock tonight. Surely, that means I have to dress appropriately." The twitch of Silas's full lips and the small crinkling at the corners of his blue eyes were the only outward signs he was amused.

"Speaking from experience, I'd say it will be your definition of appropriate that causes a challenge. In answer to your question, no, there is no uniform for the bartenders. If you are a Dom, you dress in whatever you are comfortable wearing as a dungeon monitor. Submissives dress in whatever their Dom chooses. If they don't have a Dom, they are free to choose." Carson must have read her relieved expression because he shook his head and nodded to Silas.

"Kent and Kyle delight in assigning clothing when they feel a sub has opted to play it too safe. They make sure the forum shops keep their supply closet well stocked."

"You mean they make employees wear what they give them if they don't like what they are wearing? That seems... well, it seems a lot of things, but in the interest of expediency, I'll go with highhanded." Fallon wasn't surprised when both men laughed. Hell, even as she'd spoken the words, she was embarrassed to admit how lame her outrage sounded.

"Dominants consider *highhanded* a compliment, sweetheart."

"In most cases, it's an understatement." For the first time, Fallon wondered if there was a sense of humor lurking under Carson's stern exterior. "Your clothing for this evening is already taken care of, and we'll make certain you are sorted for the next few days."

"Sorted? What exactly does that mean? And how the hell could anyone pick out something for me to wear when no one here has ever seen me?" Without thinking, Fallon unfastened her jeans and slid them to the floor, kicking them in the general direction of her discarded shirt.

"Christ in heaven, woman, you are fucking gorgeous."

Silas's whispered words sounded reverent, and her body heated in response. The tiny scrape of sheer fabric covering her bare mound would reveal every inch of what her mother always referred to as pink bits. If she was inclined to hide, it wouldn't do any good to turn around since she was wearing a thong.

"Typically, I'm not a fan of panties, but fuck me, you're well on your way to converting me."

"Turn around, Chef. I want to see if the back is as spectacular as the front." Carson's gaze moved slowly up her body, leaving goosebumps in its wake.

Their obvious appreciation fueled her courage. Turning slowly, she heard a low whistle come from where Carson stood. Hooking her fingers in the elastic at her sides, Fallon slid the garment down her thighs. Bending at the waist, she pushed them all the way to the floor, then hooked the piece of silk with a toe, sending the panties sailing atop her jeans as she stood and walked into the bathroom. Fallon couldn't remember the last time she'd felt as confident as she did hearing Carson's soft whistle.

"Hell, I'm going to need more time to decide which view I like more—that thin bit of lace bisecting her ass cheeks or those pink pussy lips begging for attention—but I know one thing. *That* is a world-class ass."

CARSON TOOK A deep breath before following Fallon into the bathroom. Giving her a quick lesson in the shower's complicated control panel, he chuckled when she let out a long-suffering sigh.

"Why must people make things so complicated? Good grief. It's just a shower, for Pete's sake. Step in, get clean, step out. Simple."

"This shower was designed for water sports, and I'm not talking about anything you'd see on ESPN." Carson caught a fleeting glimpse of her blush before she turned away, feigning interest in the recently remodeled marble wall at the back of the large enclosure. He'd sat in on the design meeting for the shower and installed the controls for the multiple showerheads. He hadn't questioned the size of the shower because he'd understood what the Wests had in mind.

"You realize this space is bigger than my living room in New York, right? You could have a party in here." He watched her eyes widen as realization dawned. "Oh, damn, I feel like a dork. I don't know why I thought reading about kink would adequately prepare me for the reality of everything involved. Everybody is going to know I'm a newbie, aren't they? This is going to be embarrassing. I just wanted to serve drinks and keep my head down until the paperwork for my license was completed." By the time she took a deep breath, Carson and Silas had already moved to flank her.

"We don't know what prompted you to move, Fallon, but we're looking forward to hearing your story. For now, let us help you adjust and enjoy your company." Carson wanted her to know they were there to help without smothering her. Typically, Silas was considered more charming, but there was something about Fallon that seemed to call to Carson's softer side. Hell, there were subs at Prairie Winds who would be shocked to hear he had a gentler side.

"My story isn't very interesting... unless you have an affinity for naïve women who seem capable of brilliantly ignoring every imaginable red flag in a relationship." Fallon sucked in a deep breath, the effect making her appear exhausted and defeated. "If it's all the same to you, I'd like to shower."

Carson noticed the chill bumps racing over the surface of her exposed skin and wanted to kick himself for not getting her under the warm water sooner.

"We'll be right outside the door if you need anything, Chef. Don't hesitate to call out if you start feeling off-kilter. When you aren't used to the intensity of Texas heat, the effects can sneak up on you." Carson wondered if her flushed cheeks were from the heat exhaustion or arousal. When the Wests asked him to act as the new bartender's tour guide, Carson had been less than thrilled. His reluctance evaporated when he realized the beauty they'd found along the road was their charge for the evening. His gaze connected with hers, and the world shifted on its axis.

Carson knew from Silas's body language, he was also interested in Fallon. Fucking hell, was it possible? Had they finally found the woman they'd been looking for? There had been times, Carson wondered if they were holding out for someone who didn't exist. Silas always assured him she was out there waiting for the two of them to show up.

"She's probably wondering where we are and what the hell is taking us so long. I understand your concern. I'm worried she will give up and settle for something that will always feel inadequate. I can't imagine anything worse than feeling as though there is more—something else just beyond your reach—but you aren't sure it's real and have no idea how to reach it."

Chapter Five

FALLON LEANED HER forehead against the cool marble shower wall and barely resisted the urge to thump her head with enough force to restart her damned brain. What the hell was she thinking, stripping in front of two men she'd only just met? Good God, she'd finally found the courage to leave a man who'd made her life hell for a year. He'd badgered her about everything, from dissecting her relationship with her deceased parents to pressuring her to move in with him. The final straw had been walking in on Hagan and a female coworker in Fallon's bed.

Her ex badgered her for months about a ménage, but Fallon wasn't interested in sharing a man with another woman. The steamy romance novels she read, where two men focused on the pleasure of a single woman, made her long to see if reality was as hot as her fantasies. Although if Hagan had suggested sharing her with one of his male friends, she probably would have turned him down— simply because the longer they dated, the less attractive she found him. The few times he'd kissed her, Fallon was disappointed her body hadn't lit up the way she'd read about in books. In the time they'd dated, Fallon hadn't had a single orgasm aside from her trusty BOB. Shaking her head, she pushed away from the wall and began shampooing her hair.

"How pathetic do you have to be to spend an entire

year dating a loser who can't even give you a damned orgasm with his fingers? I'll bet he couldn't make a woman come if he had a magic wand." Expelling the breath she didn't realize she was holding, Fallon rinsed and conditioned her hair.

Looking around, she tried to take in the opulence surrounding her, overwhelmed by the West's hospitality. They'd stocked the shower with the perfect scent for her. The white tea and sage, with undertones hinting at fresh citrus, helped clear her head and infused her with enough energy to get through the rest of the night.

"You can do this, Fallon. Be brave and enjoy the moment. They said they wanted to help, and if Lilly West says you can trust the men at the club, you need to listen to her." Rolling her eyes toward the ceiling, Fallon shut off the water and toweled the water out of her hair. "And for fuck's sake—stop talking to yourself before the men in white coats show up and haul off your crazy ass."

SILAS WAS GRATEFUL Fallon hadn't noticed they'd left the bathroom door open and couldn't hold back his smile when he heard her ex had been a lousy partner.

"It doesn't sound like it will be difficult to improve on her previous sexual experience." Carson's droll sense of humor was often difficult to interpret because he was damned good at masking his emotions, but this time, the gleam in his eyes was easy to read.

"We need to tread carefully. She is trying to talk herself into being brave, which isn't the same as feeling empowered and safe." Silas didn't want her to be theirs only for a night of experimentation. Hell, he wanted to skip the damned club tonight and spend the night locked in the apartment, learning everything he could about Fallon Foster. He wanted to know about her childhood, her favorite flower, what foods she loves, and make certain she understood her battery-operated boyfriend was no longer an option.

Silas would make it his personal mission to give Fallon everything she could hope for and more. He wanted her to experience the ecstasy of an orgasm so off the charts, it obliterated everything from her mind but the bone-melting pleasure. They hadn't invented a vibrator that could compare to what he and Carson could give her.

"She's interested in the lifestyle and ménage, although I'm not sure she is ready to admit it yet. Let's see how she does downstairs and take our cues from her reactions." When they heard the shower shut off, Carson and Silas stepped closer to the door in case Fallon called out for something they'd forgotten to set out. Lowering his voice, Carson added, "She's ours. Don't ask me how I know—I just do."

Silas wasn't surprised to hear Carson was interested in Fallon—hell, *that* was easy to see. It was out of character for Carson to look beyond one night of play and even more unusual for him to opt for caution when dealing with a sub.

Fallon hesitantly stepped into the room, wearing nothing but a towel, and Silas swore the earth stopped spinning for the few seconds it took his brain to reset. Barely tanned skin, unblemished by years of exposure to the harsh rays of the sun, spanned her slender arms and legs. He couldn't wait to feel her wrap herself around him like a second skin. He'd known her dark hair was long, but seeing the wet waves tumbling down her back, it was even longer than he'd guessed. It would be a pleasure to plait her hair before play sessions. All the pieces of her beauty were amazing in themselves, but the total was breathtaking.

When Fallon finally lifted her gaze to theirs, Silas heard Carson's quick intake of breath. He'd noticed the striking color of her eyes when they met on the side of the road, but in this light, they were truly remarkable. The icy blue color made him think of clear mountain lakes reflecting warm summer skies. Now their color was deeper, and for the first time, Silas understood what his mother meant when she'd referred to something as electric blue. It always seemed like the strangest combination of words, but the meaning was suddenly crystal clear.

"Umm, I forgot to get the clothes you said the Wests left for me."

Knowing Kent and Kyle, Silas doubted whatever they'd left would be what anyone outside the lifestyle would consider *clothes*. If Fallon was expecting something that would cover more than the barest essentials, she was in for a big surprise. Carson stepped into the closet, returning immediately with a black dress on a padded hanger. From a distance, it looked like any other cocktail dress, but Silas had seen Tobi wear something similar a few months ago and knew better.

"Where's the rest of it? That's much too short. I mean... really, they can't expect me to wear that in public. Yikes, it will barely cover my ass...ets." She was already blushing and hadn't even tried the dress on.

Silas smiled to himself—short was going to be the least of her worries.

"Drop the towel and put your hands up, Chef." There was no question Carson's instructions had been a command, but the rough tone of his voice was laced with heated desire.

Silas watched Fallon's expression, noting the shift from what was likely an internal battle between her head and her heart. It was the same struggle he knew many submissives fought until their minds understood the pleasure found in letting go.

"I can dress myself. I've been doing it for a long time. I'll just take that, and..." She reached for the hanger, but Carson moved it out of her reach. "Well, damn. Seriously? You're going to make me dress in front of the two of you?"

"No. I'm going to put this dress over your head, then Silas will braid your hair."

Silas wasn't surprised Carson had picked up on his interest in Fallon's hair. It had often been a ritual with the subs they played with when Silas wanted their hair bound. He didn't want it hiding their faces or accidentally getting caught in equipment or toys.

Fallon only hesitated a moment before dropping the towel and raising her hands over her head. It was her reaction to seeing herself in the dress that had Silas biting the inside of his cheek to keep from laughing out loud.

"Holy Mother of God. You can see through it. The whole fucking thing is sheer." The crack of Carson's palm against Fallon's almost bare ass echoed through the room, drawing a squeak from her. "What the heck was that for? Don't tell me you are offended by the f-word because I'm not falling for that... not even a little. Didn't you say you were a computer guru? That means you must have spent some time in college. Anybody who attends more than a semester has been desensitized to the word fuck." Carson's hand landed on her other ass cheek so quickly, she didn't have time to move out of the way. "What the holy heck is your problem?"

Silas had to give Carson credit. He'd wound her up enough, she'd forgotten all about her earlier issues with the dress.

"My problem is your inappropriate use of the word fuck. If you were to say, 'Sir, would you please fuck me?' for example, I'd have no complaint whatsoever with your use of the term." This time, Silas found it impossible to hold back his smile. If Fallon's glare suddenly turned deadly, Carson would be toast.

"You are joking, right? Why would I ask you to... ummm?"

"See? This is precisely the issue. You hesitate to use the term properly yet had no issue blurting it out as an expletive." At Carson's response, Fallon turned to Silas.

"Help me out here, would you? Your friend is skating on the outer rim of the sanity bell, and I'm having trouble wrapping my head around these new parameters for tour guides."

Silas had to give Fallon credit; her snark was damned witty for a woman who was being bombarded with something new and unfamiliar at every turn.

"What Carson is saying is there will be times when your profanity will not be permitted. Most Doms want their submissives to remain respectful during scenes and any time you are in the club." Silas reached forward to smooth the back of his fingers along the side of her face, tracing the column of her neck to her collarbone. "You know we're interested in you—I can see it in your eyes. Every time we touch you, your heart rate kicks up, and your breathing becomes shallow. If I had to guess, I'd say you don't understand why your body is responding to two men you just met, and you're having trouble remembering why your fantasies about ménage are supposed to be taboo."

"How?" Fallow swayed before Silas wrapped his hands around her upper arms to steady her. "How did you know? Am I that transparent? Does it make me look desperate? Hell, even I think I've lost my mind."

Rather than answer her loaded questions, Silas led her into the bathroom and began brushing her hair. Once the long strands were tangle-free, he divided the thick mass into equal parts and quickly worked the sections into a single braid. Securing it with a piece of leather he found in the drawer, he was pleased she'd remained still while he worked.

"Let's get downstairs before Kent and Kyle think we're going to keep you up here all night." As tempting as the thought was, Fallon needed to see what she was getting into—both personally and professionally. For all he knew, she might decide the whole thing was too much and walk away. She'd obviously walked away from a former lover to move to Texas, so it wasn't out of the realm of possibility she could do it again. As soon as the doors of the elevator slid closed, Fallon started to fidget.

"I can't believe you didn't let me put on underwear. Everybody and their blind grandmother will be able to see my breasts and pink bits. It's indecent. I hope I don't have to meet Ms. Lilly like this. She'll be scandalized. I don't want to embarrass her or make her think my mother was a failure. Not that my mom would ever win *Mother of the Year*, but still."

Silas looked at Carson over her head and knew his friend was thinking the same thing—Fallon was one of those wonderful subs who chattered when they were nervous. During his time as a Dom, Silas had learned to appreciate nervous chatter because there was usually a wealth of information buried in what some Masters deemed unnecessary noise. He'd seen Doms at the club punish their submissives without taking time to listen to the words... words that could easily cement the bond between them.

"Don't worry about Lilly. You won't find anyone more open-minded and accepting than Lilly West."

"Kent and Kyle are playing with Tobi tonight, so Lilly won't be here. Dean and Del won't come to the club when their sons are playing. They say they saw enough of their sons' naked backsides when they were growing up, and they don't want to violate Tobi's privacy."

Carson was right. The elder Wests were all three crazy about Tobi and went to great lengths to preserve their relationship. The two retired oilmen had built a club-worthy playroom in their home so they could continue playing without risking the obvious privacy issues with the daughter-in-law they adored.

Stepping into the club's main room, Silas closely watched Fallon's reaction and was pleased when her eyes widened with interest rather than shock or revulsion. The club's new bartender looked like a kid in a candy store, standing on tiptoe and craning her neck, making sure she didn't miss anything.

"Don't try to take it all in at once, Chef. We'll make certain you get the see anything that interests you, but first, let's stop by the bar so you can meet a few people. Members aren't allowed anything alcoholic to drink before playing, but it doesn't keep them from gathering around the bar for conversation."

"I assume there is a system for identifying someone

who's had wine or a cocktail?"

Fallon hadn't stopped straining to see the various scene areas as they walked through the main room, and Silas was impressed she was able to carry on a conversation without appearing to pay attention. Hell, maybe that wasn't such an endearing trait after all. The two of them would need to make certain she didn't become distracted during play. Smiling to himself, Silas felt confident he and Carson were up to the task.

Chapter Six

FALLON HAD BEEN so busy taking in her surroundings and trying to remember names she'd forgotten about the dress she was almost wearing until Tobi West grasped her hand, flashing a broad smile.

"Damn, girl, I have this dress, and it doesn't look this good on me. Holy Hannah, I need to start working out again now that I'm not traveling for work." The petite blonde squeaked when a man standing nearby gave her ass a solid swat. He looked nearly identical to Kent West, but there was a subtle difference in this man's demeanor, letting Fallon know they weren't one and the same.

Kyle West flashed Fallon a smile so quick, for a few seconds, she thought maybe she'd imagined it before returning his stern attention to his wife.

"Kitten, how many times have my brother and I warned you about this lapse? You will not talk negatively about yourself, or you won't sit comfortably. For the life of me, I don't understand why we suddenly seem to be back at square one on this particular issue. You are absolutely perfect, and we'll not have you insulting what belongs to us." He softened the reprimand by giving Tobi a quick kiss before turning his attention to Fallon.

"It's a pleasure to meet you, Fallon. We're happy you are here. Thank you for submitting your paperwork electronically. We have a couple of things for you to sign, but we'll take care of those details tomorrow afternoon before your shift starts. Tonight is all about getting a lay of the land and learning about your own boundaries. Silas and Carson will be able to answer any questions you might have. If, for some reason, you're not comfortable asking one of them, my brother or I will be happy to find someone else. One word of warning—some Doms are more committed to strict protocol than others, so it's important you avoid initiating a conversation with a submissive unless you are in the locker room."

Fallon knew her expression must have reflected her surprise when Tobi reached out to place her hand on Fallon's upper arm.

"Most of the members at Prairie Winds are wonderful, and they'll understand if you make a mistake, but there are a couple of Doms who would take a lot of pleasure in overseeing your punishment just because you're new. Don't hand them the opportunity."

Tobi's warning meant more than Kyle's because Fallon sensed it came from experience. Nodding her understanding, Fallon started to feel closed in by all the people surrounding her. Would she be able to fit in here? Moving so far from home suddenly seemed like a rash decision. Maybe she needed to reconsider. The idea that a stranger could have her punished was so far removed from her reality, it was hard for her to grasp the concept. Her fantasies about playful spankings that ended in mind-melting sex seemed like a childish version of the reality she'd felt Tobi was referring to. Knowing a stranger could seize the opportunity to hurt her was terrifying.

Her heart was beating so hard, she worried the two men flanking her would be able to hear it. When black dots started dancing in front of her eyes, Fallon felt warm hands moving slowly up and down the cool skin of her exposed upper arms.

"Fallon, look at me."

A vaguely familiar voice sounded like it was coming from the bottom of a well rather than from the man standing in front of her.

"Chef, you are a hot second away from being carried to the first aid station. Breathe with me." When she didn't respond, he gave her a quick shake. "Take a damned breath."

She sucked in a breath and saw relief in the man's eyes.

Carson. His name was Carson, and something about him made her think of fallen angels. His blonde hair was a couple weeks past needing a much-needed trim, making him look like the surfers she'd seen on California beaches. Fallon swore her heart seized for several beats as she remembered one of the many vacations she'd enjoyed with her parents before they died. All of their trips had been special, but their last excursion had always seemed to hold the most meaning. After her college graduation, the three of them spent a week enjoying the warm sunshine before she'd started her career. Their time walking along the colorful sidewalk of Venice Beach was the happiest and most carefree she'd ever seen them.

During one of their beach strolls, her dad reminded her they wouldn't be around forever, and she needed to be brave no matter what life threw her way.

"Someday, when your mother and I are no longer here, courage will be your greatest asset." His words were sadly prophetic—they'd died a month later.

Another breath and the fog clouding her view of Carson started to clear. He stepped to the side, making way for a second man. Silas. She remembered thinking his eyes looked like blue pools of crystal-clear water. If she looked deeply enough, would she be able to fall into their shallow depths? Did he know how captivating his eyes were? How his soul called to hers despite being virtual strangers?

"Sweetheart, my soul is drawn to yours as well."

His words surprised her since she didn't realize she'd spoken out loud.

"While Kyle and Tobi's warnings are valid, I'm asking you to trust us to guide you. We know all the members here at Prairie Winds, so we won't have any trouble keeping you safe."

Fallon pulled in a deep breath, letting Silas's reassurance smother her panic. Looking around, she was surprised to find they were no longer surrounded by other people.

"You aren't the first new member to become overwhelmed, Chef. Everyone moved back when they realized the effect the crush was having on you." Carson gave her a reassuring smile as he and Silas stepped back as well.

She knew they'd stayed close in case her knees gave out and would have appreciated their show of confidence more if it wasn't so laughable. Lord love a leper, who'd have ever thought she'd have come so close to swooning? That was the word, right? When a damsel felt utterly overwhelmed and went weak in the knees, and the hero had to steady them?

Holy shit, I really need to stop reading historical romance novels.

SILAS AND CARSON led Fallon to a small grouping of chairs behind a wall of plants, giving her a small measure of privacy while she got her feet under her again. Seeing color come back into her pale cheeks was a relief, and Silas was relieved when she started asking questions. He wasn't sure what had tipped the scales of her fear, but it was something they needed to explore. When her hands trembled, he wanted to slap his palm against his forehead.

"When is the last time you ate, sweetheart?" Fallon seemed surprised by the question, and watching her struggle to remember her last meal told them everything they needed to know.

"Jesus, Joseph, and Mary. No wonder you're struggling." Carson quickly hailed one of the trainees, giving the young man instructions to fill a plate for Fallon and bring it back as quickly as possible. The man smiled and nodded before darting across the room.

Silas knew the newbie sub would be back quickly—the man had the reputation of being almost too accommodating. Dr. Ben Stewart was an up-and-coming orthopedic surgeon at Cecelia Barnes' clinic and used his time at the club to relieve the stress of his job. Knowing his skills met CeCe's high standards and that he'd passed Cam's rigorous interview spoke volumes, but what impressed his fellow club members the most was his infectious smile and easy-going personality.

The plate Ben fixed was the perfect mix of healthy and decadent. The man might be a gifted surgeon, but he was also as submissive as anyone Silas had ever met. When Kent and Kyle mentioned they were concerned Ben's sense of self-preservation might not be at its peak in the play-room, Cam Barnes went on full alert. Cam had made it his personal mission to screen all the young physician's play partners from that point forward. Silas understood his friend's concern. Ben's need to please was strong, but looking at Fallon's plate, it was easy to see the professional side of his personality wasn't far below the surface.

"Ben, we'd like you to meet Fallon. She's new and will be working as a bartender here at Prairie Winds until her pharmacy license is successfully transferred from New York."

SILAS WAS GRATEFUL Carson made the introduction. Since their professional paths would probably cross in the future, it was a good idea to help her establish a network of contacts. The two exchanged greetings, and Ben knelt in front of Fallon's chair, so they were face to face.

"Fallon, I think your Doms introduced us because we'll almost certainly work together in the future. When your license comes through, please give me a call, and I'll put you in touch with my boss. She owns the surgical clinic and hospital where I work as an orthopedic specialist. She's mentioned establishing a pharmacy on-site. If that's something you'd be interested in, be sure to contact her. Master Silas and Master Carson can help you set it up."

Silas smiled at Ben and nodded his approval. He'd given Fallon a great tip, then handed the contact information over to the Doms. His respect for protocol was damned impressive.

Carson smiled at Ben, then surprised the man by extending his hand.

"Thanks, Dr. Stewart. We'll make certain Fallon contacts you for an introduction. I'm also going to let Kent and Kyle know how much we appreciate what you've done and how perfectly you handled the situation." The club owners would make certain Ben was properly rewarded. Ben nodded his appreciation, patting Fallon's hand as he rose to his feet.

"You're going to love it here, Fallon. There's no safer club for a submissive. The Wests always protect their members. Welcome to Prairie Winds." He gave one last nod before disappearing into the growing crowd.

Fallon cleaned the plate so quickly, Silas was tempted to make her another. When he opened his mouth to speak, she shook her head.

"I couldn't eat another bite. I'll grab a bottle of water when we walk by the bar. Can we go now? I feel like I'm taking advantage of this situation."

Silas grinned and shook his head. Damn, it was refreshing to meet someone with a solid work ethic. Ben's instincts had been dead center—Fallon would be a good match for CeCe Barnes.

"Then let's go and see what you're interested in," Carson said, holding out his hand to her.

Silas couldn't have agreed more. He was anxious to see if her interests aligned with theirs. If she used the membership privileges that were part of her employment package, she'd have already filled out the detailed interest and limits form that all potential members were required to complete. The forms listed every kink imaginable, and several most people had never considered. Doms regularly consulted the lists of new submissives before initiating a play session. Knowing if a sub's kinks were aligned with their own was an important part of their negotiations. He and Carson could learn a lot by watching Fallon's reactions when they visited various scenes, but the list would tell them even more.

The first scene station had a male sub in a slatted cage suspended approximately five feet above the floor. His

Mistress was standing to the side, chatting with friends. It might look like she was ignoring her sub, but Silas knew better. He felt Fallon shudder beside him and wasn't surprised to see the stricken look on her face.

"Why is he in a cage? Is it supposed to be some kind of punishment? He looks so sad, and no one seems to care."

He hated hearing the confusion and disillusionment in her voice.

"I would die a thousand deaths if I was subjected to that level of humiliation. I'd never show my face here again. I've felt enough humiliation to last a lifetime, and I try not to repeat mistakes." The last part was chock full of emotion.

Silas saw Carson's brow raise in unspoken question.

"Humiliation play isn't for everyone. Remember, this is a negotiated scene between a couple who have been married for many years."

Fallon's shoulders relaxed marginally at Carson's explanation, but Silas could tell she still didn't look convinced.

"It probably looks like his Mistress is ignoring him, but I can assure you that's not the case. She is tuned in to every move he makes. She'll know if his respiration rate changes, or his mood shifts away from where she's headed with the scene." Leading her away, Silas was relieved humiliation wasn't her thing since it wasn't his or Carson's either. He hoped the next scene would appeal to her because it was more in line with what they enjoyed.

Kent and Kyle stood on either side of Tobi, watching her petite form shudder from unfilled need. She was bound to a St. Andrews cross, her back to the crowd gathered around but facing a wall of mirrors. Silas knew she'd struggled with self-esteem issues related to her weight since she'd given birth to twins, but he'd assumed the problem had been addressed. Obviously, it hadn't, and it seemed her Doms were tired of reminding her what a gift she'd given them and how perfect she was in their eyes.

The little spitfire wouldn't know how many club members surrounded her until her Masters removed her blindfold. Kyle held a deer-skin flogger in one hand as he stepped closer to whisper against her ear. The club owners hadn't done a public scene in a long time, so Silas was surprised to hear his voice echo around the small space. The new lapel microphones were powerful and pro-grammed to only play over the speakers in a specific area. The new system was perfect for training—both Dominants and submissives.

"Kitten, we've told you every way we know how per-fect you are, yet you continue to disparage what belongs to us." Kyle watched his brother step forward. The wide wooden paddle in his hand didn't bode well for Tobi.

"It's damned annoying, sweetness. The ass you com-plained about earlier today is lush and fucking perfect. It's also going to be a lovely shade of crimson before we're finished." Kent rubbed the flat surface of the paddle over Tobi's bare ass cheeks.

Silas grinned when Kent's mic picked up Tobi's sigh. Carson stepped behind Fallon, wrapping an arm around her torso before pulling her back against his chest. Silas turned so he could still watch the scene playing out in front of them while monitoring Fallon's facial expressions as Carson narrated the scene in low whispers against the shell of her ear.

"Kyle's soft strokes with the flogger will feel like warm caresses. They won't hurt, but the slow build-up will bring heat that will sneak up on her." Fallon's eyes were riveted to the scene, her cheeks turning pink as the flush of arousal moved from her chest to her heart-shaped face. "They are warming her up. By the time Kent gives her the swats she's earned, she'll be floating in subspace and barely register the punishment." The truth was, this was barely a punishment. The worst for Tobi would be when she realized how many people had seen her naked backside.

Observing Fallon's reaction as Kyle increased the pace and force of the flogger strikes was every bit as arousing as the scene itself. Her face was flushed, her breathing rapid and shallow. Giving Carson a quick nod, indicating it was okay to kick things up, Silas brushed the back of his fingers over Fallon's heated cheeks before trailing them down the side of her slender neck.

"Carson is going to touch you, sweetheart. If that's a problem, now is the time to speak up." Silas loved the faraway look in her eyes. Irises that had been ice blue a few minutes ago were a deeper color now. Her pupils dilated, so only a thin ring of color remained. She looked at him, but Silas wasn't sure how much she was seeing. Damn, the woman was a textbook submissive, and learning she was a bit of a voyeur was a huge plus since they enjoyed watching scenes. Slipping their fingers or cock between a sub's slick folds as they watched a scene had led to some of the hottest sex Silas had ever experienced.

Chapter Seven

C ARSON LOVED HOW perfectly Fallon fit against him—her soft curves molding against his body, his rock-hard cock nestled between the cheeks of her ass. When she'd tried to shift forward, he'd known she hadn't missed the evidence of his arousal.

"Stay where I put you, Chef. Don't worry, my cock may be screaming for relief, but I'm capable of controlling myself." He chuckled softly before adding, "Nothing is going to happen you don't want, Fallon. Remember that. The club's safe word is red, but for tonight, all you need to say is no." Whatever Silas saw in her expression must have been unmistakable, or his friend would have never given him the go-ahead. The damned man was methodical to a fault when it came to submissives.

Carson wrapped his hand around her, sliding up the few inches of bare thigh above the hem of her short dress. Her toned thighs quivered beneath his fingertips, and he smiled at her quick intake of breath. She shuddered in his arms, sagging for a heartbeat before stiffening her spine. He hadn't even made his way to her pussy and could already smell the earthy scent of her arousal. Damn, he was eager to feel her cream coating his fingers.

"Are you wet for me, Chef?" She unconsciously opened her legs, giving him the small space he needed to push through her wet folds. "Fuck me, you're drenched. You have no idea how much that pleases me. Knowing you're turned-on, watching Tobi's Masters send her so far into subspace, she couldn't tell you her own name, is damned near perfect. Tell us what you see, sweetheart."

It was human nature to comment on the most meaningful elements first, so they'd take note of those first observations. Whatever stood out to her would give them a lot of insight into her interests.

"When I was introduced to Tobi, she was so vivacious and welcoming. Seeing her now, you would never know it was the same woman."

"What do you think the difference is, sweetheart?" Silas agreed with Fallon. Even with her eyes covered, Tobi's facial expression was easy to read—she was lost in the moment.

"She doesn't care about anyone other than Kent and Kyle. You may think she doesn't realize there's a crowd gathered around, but she does. It simply doesn't matter to her, which I don't think is her usual way of dealing with people."

Carson looked at Silas, who was staring back with a *what the fuck* expression Carson understood too well. How in the hell had she seen so much in such a short time? The woman's instincts were dead-on. She'd seen more than either of them noticed.

"Damn, Fallon, your insight is remarkable." When her cheeks turned a sweet pink, Carson made a mental note to compliment her often, so it would feel normal rather than being a cause of embarrassment. He'd never understood men who expected their wives and girlfriends to worship the ground they walked on when the fools rarely spoke a kind word to their women.

They continued to watch the scene until Kyle and Kent carried their limp sub off to a private room. Watching Tobi's lack of response when the blindfold was removed was proof Fallon had been right. As they walked to the adjoining scene, Silas paused, turning Fallon so they were face to face.

"How many scenes have you observed, sweetheart? Were you a member of a kink club in New York?"

Carson wanted to smile at Silas's blunt questions. His friend was usually the smooth one, leaving Carson the role of boorish rogue. *Damn, I may have to turn over a new leaf. I could get used to being the suave one.*

"Two, counting the one we just watched. No kink club membership. I haven't been out of college very long, and while I was in school, I was too busy working and studying to have a social life. I went to class, studied, and worked… that's it."

Since Carson's wealth was entirely self-made, he understood when she said she hadn't had time for extra-curricular activities. He'd worked his way through school until it became clear a piece of parchment wouldn't help him enough to devote another two years pursuing it. Dropping out of college and starting his own company sent his extended family into a tailspin. He didn't think his grandfather would ever stop raging, but when Carson's business took off a few months later, the elderly man finally admitted a diploma didn't matter.

The next scene was a wax demonstration, and Carson almost burst out laughing when he heard Fallon whisper, "Nope, nope, and nope. I worked a bunch of extra hours so I could afford laser treatments. Hot wax and skin should never meet."

"You let a technician laser your tender bits, Chef?" he

said against her ear, making certain no one else was privy to his inquiry. Interrupting a scene with idle chatter was rude and considered a breach of club protocol. He had no intention of being called before the owners for something every member knew was unacceptable. Fallon nodded as she shuddered. Moving along, Carson couldn't resist teasing her a bit. "I'm looking forward to hearing what made you choose laser treatments and what fueled your aversion to waxing. I know there are advantages and disadvantages to both."

As tight as money must have been for her, deciding to have expensive laser treatments brought several questions to mind. When she'd stripped in front of them upstairs, Carson assumed her smooth pussy was the result of a recent trip to a spa. His train of thought was derailed by Fallon's soft gasp.

"That's low-temp wax, right? Please tell me it's not regular wax. Holy crap on a cactus, did you see that? He dripped wax over her nipple." She'd unconsciously pulled her hands up to cover her breasts, but Carson intercepted the move. Wrapping his hands around her delicate wrists, he pulled her arms behind her. Securing them with one hand, he leaned forward to press a kiss against her temple.

"Keep your hands where I put them, Chef. Silas and I are enjoying the view. Seeing your nipples draw up into tight peaks is your body's way of telling us you are more interested in the scene than your mind is ready to admit." He felt her stiffen against him and chuckled. "Don't get your back up, Fallon. It's common for a submissive's body to be way ahead of their head. Hell, even experienced subs struggle with this from time to time. You might think the internal battle would be related to the perceived level of pain, but that's not necessarily the case."

"The more likely answer is the conflict is related to the messages society bombards us with our entire lives." Silas moved closer, ensuring his words wouldn't be heard beyond their tight circle. "The stricter a family's perception of acceptable, the more difficult it is to resolve the difference. Take me, for example. I was raised in a hippy commune, where acceptable sexual behavior had a very broad definition. As a matter of fact, the only rules in my hometown mirror the guiding tenet of every reputable kink club I've ever visited. *Safe, sane, and consensual* is more than a motto, sweetheart. It is the basis of every scene, whether or not it ends in sex."

The explanation Silas gave was accurate, but Carson wasn't sure Fallon heard enough to make it meaningful.

"Gracie's men know her body better than she does, and they are giving her what she desires most."

"Men?"

Carson knew she'd spoken louder than intended but felt obligated to address the misstep, anyway. Giving her ass a quick slap, he was pleased when her gaze immediately dropped.

"I'm sorry. I was just so surprised when you implied there was another Dom involved."

"Look at the tall man standing to the left." Carson knew she wouldn't miss Jax McDonald. An inch shy of seven-foot, the man was damned hard to overlook. Jax winked at her, clearly amused by her response at discovering Gracie was involved in a poly-relationship. Carson felt her relax slightly and gave Jax a grateful nod. "You'll be working with Jax and Micah. They head up the security team tasked with keeping everyone safe at the club and on the surrounding property."

"Carson made the distinction of the club and immediate property because the teams of special contract operators have their own leaders. We aren't trying to overwhelm you, but every layer of information will help when you are introduced to people." Silas understood how overwhelming the well-meaning members of the club could be when someone new joined the crew.

The turnover was extremely low because the Wests were ordinarily meticulous during the hiring process, which was one of the things that made Fallon's hiring so unusual. Neither Carson nor Silas had been consulted for a security clearance prior to Fallon's hiring because of her personal connection to the West family. Ordinarily, they'd have helped with her background check and would already be armed with information.

"Jax is responsible for the beautiful rope work securing Gracie to the table. Micah isn't a huge fan of hot wax, but there isn't anything he wouldn't do for his wife." Carson agreed both men were completely devoted to Gracie. Even though Jax was the first one to meet Gracie, Micah Drake is equally enthralled.

"Imagine having two men focused on your pleasure. Two men who believe your trust is their greatest treasure." If Carson hadn't been holding her, he might have missed the shiver skittering up her spine. He'd bet his considerable fortune, Fallon had already fantasized about ménage. It was his and Silas's job to make her wildest dreams a reality.

Carson wanted nothing more than to head upstairs and spend the rest of the evening getting to know Fallon much more intimately. They'd start in the elevator, stripping her, so their view of her world-class ass wasn't obscured as she walked into the apartment. It seemed odd to think how much his mindset had changed in a few hours. He and Silas often wondered if a polyamorous relationship was in their future—worried they were looking for a woman who didn't exist. He hadn't been sure they'd ever agree about a woman, but Fallon had changed everything.

As they walked through the main room, Fallon relaxed more the further they went. He wondered if she was becoming somewhat desensitized to what was happening around her, or she was envisioning herself in the scenes. Perhaps she was wondering what it would feel like to be paddled or flogged. By the time they'd circled the room, Carson could see she was fading. When she tripped over the edge of a throw rug, he and Silas knew it was time to get her upstairs.

As they led Fallon to the elevators, Silas sent a quick text to Kent, letting him know they were calling it a night and promising to touch base first thing in the morning. Before the elevator doors were sealed, Carson asked her if she needed something to eat before bed. She shook her head, but he turned her, so they were face to face.

"You're always expected to answer with words, Chef. Dominance and submission rely on trust and communication. While the first is earned, it's dependent on the second. If you answer with words, we will all have a better chance of getting it right."

She nodded but quickly caught herself.

"I understand. It's always that way in the books I've read. No, I'm not hungry, but thank you for asking. It's been a long day. Since I didn't have to work behind the bar tonight, I think my body has decided to shut down early. I'm not sure what's happening. I can usually work a double shift without thinking twice."

"When was the last time you slept? And cat naps in

your car do not count, Chef." Carson didn't like the way her brow furrowed as she considered her answer. *If you have to think that hard to remember when you slept last, it has been too damned long.*

"Probably before I left New York. I didn't want to waste money on motel rooms since I don't know how long my ex can hold up my license transfer. Honestly, I have no idea why he cares. He didn't seem terribly alarmed when I walked into my apartment and found him in bed with one of the nineteen-year-old clerks from the store where I worked. And inviting me to join them? Ewww." It was the first time she'd alluded to why she'd left so abruptly.

After seeing the interest in her eyes downstairs each time they'd stopped to watch a ménage scene, it wasn't hard to imagine her sharing her interest with the man she was dating. She'd entrusted him with information, and the jackass probably used it in a way that benefited him rather than met the needs of the woman he was supposed to care for—selfish bastard.

"We're going to have a long conversation about your ex, sweetheart, but I think it's a conversation for tomorrow. Tonight, we'd like to play a bit, then make sure you get a good night's sleep."

Carson appreciated Silas stepping up when he'd been too distracted to mention their intentions.

"We don't want to overwhelm you, but we will begin as we intend to go." Stopping in the middle of the spacious apartment, Silas turned Fallon toward him and kept his hands wrapped around her upper arms.

"First, a few ground rules. We are both interested in pursuing what appears to be a mutual attraction. If that isn't the case, you need to say something now." Fallon's shy smile and deep blush was all the answer needed, but it was important for her to respond.

"I'm interested, although I feel foolish since it doesn't make sense for me to jump out of the frying pan into the fire."

Carson was impressed. Her response was perfect. Not only was she interested, she understood the need for caution.

"We understand and will respect any boundaries you set, but be aware, we will push you. Hell, every Dom I know is a pushy bastard who enjoys showing a submissive the pleasure that lies just outside their comfort zone." Carson was known for pushing submissives. He often pushed them too far, too fast, sending them scurrying back to the comfort of the unattached subs area of the club.

"I'm not as shy and retiring as I might have first appeared. I'll speak up if I'm not comfortable or need a break. I assume Prairie Winds uses the stoplight system?" Carson and Silas smiled. It was obvious Fallon hadn't been kidding when she claimed to have read about the lifestyle.

After the explosion of erotic romance books flooded the market, Carson did enough research to know they were usually fairly accurate on a few points and one hundred eighty degrees out on everything else. The basics, like safe words and the stoplight system to assess a submissive's comfort level, were usually explained fairly well. It was the internal struggle subs experienced when giving up the control he'd found glossed over at best and completely misrepresented at worst.

It was going to be interesting to see how easily she transitioned from fictional submission to reality.

Chapter Eight

WAKING UP ALONE in bed the next morning, it took every ounce of Fallon's self-control to keep from slapping her palm against her forehead. What on earth was she thinking, getting involved with two men she'd only met a few hours earlier? Sure, they'd been personally selected by Lilly West and her sons, and in Fallon's estimation, recommendations didn't come any higher, but still. At this point, she didn't trust her own judgment. Fucking hell, maybe it was smarter to rely on Lilly's.

She silently vowed to enjoy what they offered and learn everything she could during the short time she was here. As soon as she found a pharmacy position, Fallon would rent a small apartment and start over. Damn, it pissed her off to think about all the money she'd lost leaving so suddenly. Hopefully, her landlord would forward her security deposit, and her former employer would send her last paycheck—although since Hagan's family owned the chain of stores she'd worked for, it didn't seem likely.

Letting Silas and Carson know she was interested didn't mean she wanted a full-blown relationship, damn it. She had as much right as anyone else to play a little without thinking it would last forever. Since she'd worked her ass off during college, Fallon missed all the wild parties and opportunities for one-night stands her friends experienced. Hagan called her a dick tease, a description she didn't feel she'd earned. After all, there had to be other women who flirted without bedding every man they encountered.

She'd been introduced to several men and seen countless others this evening, but none of them had interested her beyond wondering what they did for a living or how they fit into the hierarchy of the club. The two men who had been standing in front of her were entirely different. She'd felt electricity pulse between herself and Silas from the moment she looked into his eyes on the side of the road. Carson provided another surge of unexplained heat, and she'd wondered if her soul had recognized them when her head knew they were strangers.

Sitting up, Fallon noticed a folded sheet of paper on the nightstand with her name printed in neatly penned block letters on the front. Opening it, she forced the sleep from her eyes, trying to focus on the writing.

Hope you caught up on a bit of rest. Take your time getting ready for the day. We're looking forward to showing you around, but we needed to take care of a few things at work. Wear what is set out on the bathroom counter—nothing more, nothing less. S & C

Getting to her feet, Fallon was shocked to see the sun had not only risen, but it was also already high enough to be casting a long shadow under the eaves. *Damn, what the hell time is it, anyway?* Looking around the room for a clock, she wondered how anyone knew what time it was. She'd heard the pace of life in Texas was slower, but people still needed alarm clocks. Moving around the room, she grinned when she noticed a pillow propped in front of a large clock radio. Someone had gone to a lot of effort to make certain she wouldn't be embarrassed by how long she'd slept.

Ha! Shows what they know. I never apologize for sleeping. Hell, a good night's sleep is a gift from the angels. Being able to escape into sleep helped save my sanity after my parents died.

Taking care of business, then hopping in the shower, she hadn't taken time to check out the clothing on the counter until she'd dried her hair. Holding up the skimpy piece of fabric some designer probably called a dress, Fallon chuckled. If she sneezed, she was definitely going to flash anyone paying attention, and heaven forbid if there was a breeze.

"Crap, it's windy in Texas, right?" Checking the floor before rechecking the expansive countertop, she wondered where they'd left her bra and panties.

Fallon was so lost in her own thoughts she didn't register Silas moving until his palm covered hers to pull the flimsy dress out of her hand. The warmth of his other hand settled over the cool skin of her ass cheek, a heartbeat before a heated slap sent a rush of heat through her entire body. She wasn't sure what she'd done wrong, and judging by her body's reaction, he would likely need to find another form of punishment. Lifting her gaze to meet his in the mirror, she raised a brow in question but didn't speak the question aloud.

"Much better. Another important rule of any D/s dynamic is safety, which includes situational awareness. You had no idea I was anywhere nearby. What if I'd been an intruder? Dominants are selfish bastards. Not only do we believe your full attention is our due, we also want you safe at all times and will go to great lengths to make sure you learn the lesson. Until we gain your compliance, there will be consequences."

"Sometimes Silas' hippy psycho-babble background bubbles up to the surface, making it easy to get lost in the word salad." Carson was leaning against the door jamb, arms crossed over his chest with one leg propped casually in front of the other.

Damn, the man should be gracing the covers of magazines. He watched as her gaze moved to his bare forearms, the long sleeves of his Oxford shirt rolled up to reveal a hint of the ink she'd traced with the tip of her tongue last night. The rogue gave her a conspiratorial grin.

"It boils down to this. Pay attention. Daydreaming can cause too many problems to get into right now. You're a smart woman, so it won't take you long to sort it out."

After what she'd seen downstairs the night before, it wasn't difficult to see why it was important for all participants in a scene to remain focused.

"You experienced one of the advantages of a ménage last night. Having two men whose sole purpose is your pleasure guarantees you'll have very little time to become distracted. We'll make it our mission to keep you in the moment, but learning to be situationally aware is on you. We can give you pointers, but ultimately, you'll need to stay alert."

Silas still had his hand under her dress, the warmth of his hand pressed against her stinging cheek letting the heat sink all the way to her core. He was watching her closely, and Fallon squirmed at the intensity of his gaze.

"You're so responsive, sweetheart. A simple touch makes your pupils dilate until there is nothing left but the thinnest ring of color."

"Let's remind you how sweet it is to be touched by two men." Carson moved to her side and slipped his hand under the hem, his fingertips brushing over the top of her mound. Fallon's knees threatened to fold out from under her, and the slightest sway was enough to have the men close the space between them. "Your responses are perfect. Having you naked between us is something we'll always look forward to. Your pulse is pounding at the base of your neck, and your respiration has kicked up. Fucking perfect. If we don't get out of here now, we won't get out of this apartment until it's time for you to go to work."

Fallon wasn't sure what was the most potent—their words or touch. The surge of heat moving through her settled between her thighs, and she hoped they didn't notice the moisture coating the sensitive folds of her pussy. Damn, if they didn't move things along, it was going to trickle down her leg, and she would die of mortification. She could see the headline now: *Newly Hired Bartender at Local Kink Club Expires from Wet Pussy Embarrassment.*

"Wet pussy embarrassment? I'm not sure I've ever heard of that particular affliction. Why would you be embarrassed by something we consider a goal? Now, let's switch gears and move downstairs. We'll take a walk around the grounds to make certain you know all the security features of the property. We've ordered a late lunch and will eat by the pool. You'll still have time to rest before your shift tonight. Tobi and Lilly are out for the day, so we won't worry about anyone dropping by the pool."

Fallon was having trouble tracking the conversation with their devious fingers dancing over her bare skin. *Damn, I knew this dress was too short.*

"I agree, and as much as I've enjoyed the view of your rosy nipples peaking beneath the silky fabric, I think it will look even better on the pool deck. Let's go, Chef."

An hour later, Fallon walked through an ornate gate leading to one of the most beautiful pool areas she'd ever seen. She gasped, making both men chuckle in response.

"The rest of the property is beautiful, and the landscaping looks like something you'd see in a magazine, but it was easy to see every detail was dictated by security. I'm looking forward to seeing what it looks like at night with all the pretty lights no one thought I noticed."

Both men laughed as they led her to a table nestled against a sky-high hedge. The salad luncheon was perfect after they'd walked so far in the oppressive heat. She might have started out frustrated about the skimpy dress, but it didn't take her long to appreciate their foresight.

"Oh, I forgot to thank you for the sneakers." She'd been surprised to discover they had a pair of comfortable shoes for her to wear.

"Darlin', your shoes weren't suited for what we planned. I admit they aren't the most fashionable footwear available, but comfort is the name of the game when you're slated to be on your feet most of the night."

She agreed with Carson that comfort trumps fashion when your job requires you to stand for extended periods of time. As a pharmacist, she was used to being on her feet, but tending bar in college had been a brutal wake-up call the first night when she'd worn snazzy heels with her skinny jeans. It had taken over a week for the blisters to heal. Lesson learned.

"If you're finished, there is something we'd like to show you." The gleam in Carson's eyes should have served as a warning; instead, it made her giddy with anticipation.

Placing her hand in his outstretched one, Fallon let him lead her around the deck to a private space behind a sheet of water falling over a two-story rock wall. The soothing sound she'd enjoyed during lunch was much more intense in this small space, as if the designers had intentionally created two distinct functions from something so incredibly simple.

Fallon knew Silas was behind her, even though he'd remained quiet, letting Carson take the lead. She was impressed with how seamlessly they worked together and wondered how many long-term relationships they'd had where they shared a woman. Pushing the question to the back of her mind, Fallon repeated her silent vow to learn what she could and enjoy each day as it came.

Take in what you enjoy and freely walk away from anything that doesn't feed your soul.

Her parents' deaths forever altered her worldview in ways she'd never expected, but their lessons still echoed through her soul. One of their oft-repeated refrains was reminding her to value every moment. It was that lesson that helped her walk away from Hagan without a second thought. His cheating might have been the catalyst, but it wasn't the only reason she'd left. He'd worked tirelessly to make her feel inferior, and her self-esteem had been battered but not broken. Hagen Brody was a mistake she'd never make again.

"I know one thing for certain about your ex, Chef. He was a fool to let you go." Carson's simple compliment made her eyes burn with unshed tears as emotion welled up inside her. "I don't want to waste our limited time this afternoon or this lovely space thinking about an idiot. Let's redirect our attention to how sweet I thought your dress would look fluttering to the pool deck."

She watched his nostrils flare and wondered if he could smell her arousal. God in heaven, she wondered *again* if Carson and Silas could make her come from their words alone.

"Lose the dress, Chef."

Fallon pushed the spaghetti straps off her shoulders and let the garment glide over her curves before it fluttered to the stamped concrete pool deck.

"I was right. It looks better pooled around your feet."

"I hate to point out the obvious, but you aren't looking at the dress." He hadn't looked at the damned dress once since it passed her breasts on its rapid trip south. Carson's gaze moved slowly back to her face, a knowing smile spreading over his face.

"Nope. Don't need to. Who the hell cares about a dress when they have a gorgeous naked woman standing in front of them? A woman whose entire body is telegraphing need and a soul-deep desire to find out what she's been missing. Seeing worry pushed back by a leap of faith is all any man can ask for. Believe me, Chef, there's never been a dress made that can compete with the beauty of courage."

Fallon felt the familiar burn of tears stinging the back of her eyes but was determined to keep them from spilling over. She'd always been more emotional when happy than sad, a trait few other people understood.

"Eyes on me, Chef."

Fallon didn't realize she'd dropped her gaze to the floor and recognized awareness in Carson's expression.

"You aren't used to being complimented, are you? Hell, why am I asking when I already know the answer?"

Silas stepped around her to stand shoulder to shoulder with Carson.

"Sweetheart, what Carson is trying to say is he and I will do everything possible to make sure you're safe, well cared for, and happy. We've spent many hours discussing the kind of woman we want to share our life with, and every conversation has started with finding a partner who is committed to being courageous enough to take a chance. An adventurous spirit is intoxicating to men whose professional lives often operate on adrenaline. Yours is particularly appealing because it's edged with a desire to explore and learn. Seeing everything through your eyes will be a huge turn-on for us."

"Enough chit-chat. We can wax poetic tomorrow. Let's move this along before some damned romance writer shows up to take notes, and we never get to the fun part."

Fallon snickered at Carson's irreverence, but at the same time, she was thrilled he'd broken through the tension. Framing her face in his large hands, Carson tilted her head to the side before sealing his lips over hers. The move caught Fallon by surprise. She'd expected Silas to be the one to make the first move. The kiss shifted from sweet to passionate to possessive in the blink of an eye.

Feeling as if she was floating, just before her back pressed against the cool rock wall, Fallon was surprised when Carson pulled her back enough to slip his hand between her tender skin and the rough stone. She lost herself in Carson's kiss and knew she must have looked dazed when he finally pulled back.

"Nothing better than a kiss so hot, your woman doesn't know she's being moved into the perfect position."

Fallon's breath caught when she turned to look at Silas, wondering how he'd known. His eyes blazed with an unmistakable desire so hot, she'd have sworn heat radiated around him.

"There will be times we'll ask you to undress and present yourself to us. There are a lot of different positions Doms ask their submissives to learn. Not everyone uses the same names for the poses, and there are subtle differences. For now, we'll take charge and move you into position, but later tonight, we'll begin teaching you about the poses we consider important. For example, when told to present yourself, we simply want you to stand with your feet shoulder-width apart. Keep your chin level with the floor and your attention centered on us." Carson let her slide down his chest until her feet were once again on the damp concrete, then put his foot between hers, moving her left foot out several inches, and used his fingers to lift her chin.

"You're beautiful, Fallon." Silas skimmed the back of his fingers from the outside of her shoulder down to her elbow. "We'll enjoy looking at you, and it gives us a chance to see how you react to verbal and physical stimulation. The tremble of the toned muscles beneath your skin when I touch you is perfect. Last night, as we walked around the club, I loved the hitch in your breath when a submissive found their release. The soft sighs as you watched Doms carry their sweet subs off for aftercare made me want you even more. All in all, watching you look on as club members played was an exercise in frustration."

This was the first time Fallon suspected there was an edge to Silas. She felt like she'd been given a hint there was a will of steel beneath the laid-back exterior.

"Submissives don't always understand the importance of inspections, viewing them as intimidation or humiliation. You will never need to question why we've given this particular command because we'll tell you. It might be something as simple as seeing how your body responded to an earlier scene. We don't want to leave marks that last longer than a few hours. As a pharmacist, you are in a position of trust, and we don't want you to be forced to make excuses for unexplained bruises."

Carson's comments surprised her. The only boyfriend she'd ever had couldn't have given a tinker's damn about her reputation in the community. The truth was, she hadn't considered how difficult it would be to work in the Texas heat wearing a turtleneck and long sleeves to hide marks like the ones she'd seen last night. Rolling her eyes at her own naivety, Fallon felt the energy shift around her and wondered if a storm was brewing.

"What was that thought, Chef? Before you answer, let me remind you, editing and censoring are tantamount to lying by omission. The only way a polyamorous relationship can thrive is if we're totally honest with each other."

"Damn, this is embarrassing. I wasn't trying to be disrespectful to you. I was rolling my eyes because it's humbling to realize how much I don't know. It never occurred to me I might have to wear long sleeves and turtlenecks in the scorching heat to hide marks. I can just see the looks I'd get from my geriatric patients. The ladies would be scandalized, and the old men would get stiffies, then die from lack of oxygen to their brains. Oh yes, indeed. Let's all welcome Fallon Foster to Texas. The newbie kinkster showed up at Drugs R Us and knocked off four old farts and pissed off the President of the Altar Society before lunch."

Fallon wasn't sure when she'd moved, but when she realized her mistake, she froze in her tracks. They'd been explaining inspections, and even though they hadn't specifically mentioned standing still, she was fairly certain pacing the length of the waterfall, waving her arms around like pinwheels as she went off on a tangent, wasn't acceptable. Good grief, they probably wished they'd left her on the side of the road. Maybe she should plead temporary insanity based on a delayed reaction to a closed head injury. Granted, it was lame, but it might be her best shot.

"Damn, I said that all out loud, didn't I?"

Chapter Nine

S ILAS COULDN'T HOLD back his laughter. Fallon was perfect for them. It seemed the Universe had been listening to their litany of requests after all. She was bright, interested in the lifestyle, witty, and gorgeous. There wasn't a doubt in his mind she was going to be fast friends with Tobi and the other submissives at the club. He couldn't wait until they organized a 'Welcome to the Crew' party for her. If he had to guess, Silas would put his money on a soiree already being planned. Tobi and Gracie never missed an opportunity to host a party for their friends.

I wonder if they'd be willing to take suggestions. A pool party sounds excellent. The subs always end up naked, and all the Doms do is show up and pluck their wayward, horny women out of the water.

"You are amazing, sweetheart. Your sense of humor is perfectly aligned with ours. You and Tobi are going to be great friends." When he saw her shoulders relax, Silas realized how much his bark of laughter had alarmed her.

"While the two of you chit-chat, I'm going to stand right here and enjoy the view. Hell, I'm not sure I've ever enjoyed a mini-rant more." Carson's words were all it took for Fallon to remember she was naked.

Silas bit the inside of his cheek to keep from smiling when her eyes went wide, and she looked frantically around her in a futile attempt to make certain no one was watching. She'd learn soon enough, someone was always watching at Prairie Winds—every nook and cranny of the damned place was wired for sight and sound.

When she bent to retrieve her dress, Carson shook his head and growled, "Don't even think about it." They needed to make it clear they didn't want her hiding what they were rapidly considering theirs.

"I derailed this whole encounter, didn't I? I swear I could submarine a battleship without even trying. Maybe we should just call it a day. I'll go upstairs and get ready for work, and we can give it another shot tomorrow. How many bedrooms are in the Wests' apartment? There must be several. The place is huge. Do you live nearby, or would you prefer to stay in a guest room? Or I can move to a smaller room, and you can have the main suite."

Fallon's sudden look of awareness told Silas she'd recognized how disconnected she sounded. He saw Carson smile when she clamped her mouth shut. This was the sort of thing Carson lived for—the challenge of keeping up with a running commentary was a game he excelled at, so Silas need only stand back and enjoy the show.

"No. I doubt it. No. Four. Indeed, it is. Yes. Not a chance. Not necessary."

Fallon stood mute, blinking as her mind scrambled to remember the questions she'd ask and match them to the answers Carson rattled off. Silas fought to keep a straight face as she sorted through the jumble of words, but Carson made no attempt to hide his amusement.

"We are not that easy to shake, Chef. If we were *derailed* by every little distraction, we'd be poor businessmen and pathetic Doms. You will have to go a lot further over the edge to discourage us." She started to respond, but Carson's pointed look had the desired effect, silencing any protest she'd planned to voice.

"Enough talking. We'll have plenty of time to rehash everything later… a lot later. Back in position, sweet sub, and do yourself a favor and stop thinking." Silas wasn't sure Fallon fully understood how much strength it took to submit.

"True submission relies on trust, Fallon. As we spend more time together, you'll learn to trust us, and you'll become more confident in ways you can't begin to understand now. And we'll learn to trust you. Remember, we are relying on your honesty to help us meet all your needs." Seeing the light of understanding flash in her eyes, Silas was relieved she wasn't becoming so lost in the details that she'd lost sight of the end goal. It only took her a few seconds to get back into position, the upward tilt of her chin hinting at the confidence he'd mentioned earlier.

"Perfect. Damn, I love quick studies. Your posture is regal. Your position is perfect."

Silas could hear the admiration in Carson's voice. His friend was damned hard to impress, and Fallon was blowing them away at every turn.

Trailing the pads of his fingers down her arm, Carson smiled when her nipples drew into peaks so tight, Silas wasn't surprised to see her shift her shoulders forward a fraction of an inch before self-correcting. New subs were often shocked by their body's reactions. Professional women were accustomed to being in control, and discovering their bodies responded, no matter if their head was on board, was alarming at first. Subs mentioned how eye-opening and humbling the experience was in the beginning.

It had taken Silas longer than some to understand how submissives could be so enslaved by social mores. He'd always be grateful his parents raised him to be open-minded and to disregard society's narrow parameters in favor of following his heart. The small enclave where he'd grown up was filled with the least judgmental people he knew. Over the years, the community's mantra shifted from 'Do what makes you feel *good'* to 'Do what you know is *right.'* The oft-repeated lesson served him well as a Dom, and he made it his mission to help others break free from the cumbersome rules they often felt obligated to abide by and live the life they deserve.

FALLON WASN'T SURE where she found the courage to stand naked—outside, for heaven's sake—in front of two men she'd only just met. Her body seemed to have disconnected from her brain. *Probably grew tired of your annoying habit of overanalyzing things.* Her parents had often tried to get her out of her own head, even going so far as taking her to see the locations where her favorite books were set. They'd floated down the Mississippi River on a paddleboat when she read *Huckleberry Finn* and *Tom Sawyer* and walked the streets of London, picturing what it looked like when Pip would have walked the cobblestone streets. Smiling to herself, Fallon remembered reading *Great Expectations* so many times, the pages started falling out of her book.

Their last trip had been a few months before they died. The whole trip was surreal because it centered around *The DaVinci Code*, but her parents focused more on The Rose Line and cryptex puzzles than Paris. Before they returned home, her dad had taken her out for coffee. It wasn't unusual for her to spend time with her parents individually, but something about his behavior that morning seemed off. She hadn't been able to pinpoint the problem, but she still remembered the odd feeling she'd had the whole time they'd been alone.

After finding a secluded booth, her dad slid a long, slender box across the table and gave her a nervous smile she noted hadn't reached his eyes. It was the one time she'd felt completely unnerved being alone with her dad. Fallon and her mother often butted heads as mothers and daughters often do, but she'd always felt as though she and her dad were two sides of the same coin. When she started to untie the ribbon, he'd stilled her hands and asked her to save it for a time when she felt particularly alone.

Before she could ask any of the questions racing through her mind, his phone rang. He was called away for an emergency at work, and Fallon was left to return home with her mom. It was the last time she saw them alive. They'd talked on the phone, but she'd never gotten another chance to feel their arms wrap around her or the comfort of being pulled into hugs that felt like the safest place in the world. Fallon didn't realize she was crying until Carson lifted her chin, forcing her to meet his concerned eyes.

"Talk to us, Fallon. Where did you go, and what made you cry?"

Good grief, what on earth had she done? They were going to triple-bill her as a nut case, trouble magnet, and emotional train wreck... oh yeah, she was off to a great start.

"I started off wondering where I found the courage to stand naked in front of two men I just met because this is very out of character for me. Then I worried I was overanalyzing things." She couldn't hold back her giggle when they pasted on the phoniest shocked expressions she'd ever seen. "Don't give up your day jobs. I don't see Academy Awards in your immediate future." She relaxed when she realized they'd done exactly what they'd intended—break the tension from a few seconds earlier. "Long story short, I ended up remembering the last trip I took with my parents and the strange way it ended. My dad gave me a puzzle and told me to save it until a time I felt most alone. In some ways, it seemed as if he was telling me to keep it until they were gone."

Shaking her head at yet another peculiar shift in the energy around her, Fallon couldn't imagine getting things back on track until she felt Silas kiss the top of her shoulder. The soft brush of his lips over her skin made her gasp. The simple touch was all it took for her to feel as though her skin was being electrified from the inside, and every cell in her body was suddenly alert and ready for more.

"So responsive. Your soft sighs and quick inhalations speak volumes, sweetheart," Silas whispered against the sensitive spot behind her ear. The warm brush of air sent goosebumps racing down her arms. "We'll talk about the puzzle and explore what it might mean after we enjoy the rest of our afternoon. You have a full evening in front of you, and things will look entirely different after a good night's sleep."

"And nothing ensures a great shift at work and a good night's rest better than a few off-the-chart orgasms."

A few? Is he serious? She'd worked hard for every release her little pink vibrator gave her. Hell, even with it working at top speed, she'd never been guaranteed to find her release.

"A few? That seems a bit... ummm, well, optimistic."

Stuttering her response had made her sound sexually inexperienced when she'd wanted them to see her as sophisticated. Well, hell, she probably had a snowball's chance in hell fooling them, so she wasn't sure why she was making an effort. Might as well be honest.

"Let me guess, orgasms required so much work, they eventually didn't seem worth the effort." This time it was Carson tantalizing her with a touch so tender it reminded her of a warm summer breeze.

She caught herself leaning closer before reluctantly re-suming the proper position. Fallon wasn't sure how he'd known, but she suspected she wasn't the only woman who'd ever faced this dilemma. When she realized how many women the two of them had topped, something too close to jealousy stirred inside her. Carson immediately pulled back and locked his eyes on hers.

"Tell me what you were thinking just now. Don't lie because I'll know. Your mind went someplace unpleasant, and I want to know where so we can avoid this trigger in the future."

Fallon had always been an open book, and more often than not, it landed her in hot water. Growing up, she tried to focus on what her mom called 'the grace of being saved from long-term heartache,' but Fallon had never quite been able to convince herself it was worth it. Pulling in a deep breath, she forged ahead. They might as well find out now that she had a possessive streak, and the ugly trait might be a mile wide where they were concerned.

"I wondered how you'd known, then it occurred to me, the two of you must have had a lot of experience with women, and that didn't sit well. I know I don't have any claim on you, and even if I did, you can't change your past, but sometimes logic doesn't prevail." By the time she finished, the corners of Carson's lips were quirking up, and his gray eyes were dancing with delight.

"Thank you for being honest. There are a couple of things I'd like to address, but first, I want you to know it pleases me more than you know to hear you didn't like the thought of Silas or me being with other women. While it's true, we have a lot of experience, we are also older than you, so by default, we've had more opportunities. Playing with a submissive at the club doesn't always end with sex, although we have always tried to make sure the woman who put herself in our care was well satisfied at the end of the evening. The women we've talked to have consistently told us their biggest hurdle was being brave enough to open themselves up to new experiences. Having them explain the struggle between what their bodies wanted and what their heads were insisting was proper helped us recognize it and similar issues in others."

"Think of it as paying it forward, if you will."

Fallon wasn't sure when Silas moved or when... holy crap on a cactus, the man was shirtless. His upper body was a piece of sculpted art. *The Renaissance Masters must rejoice in heaven every time he undresses.* Silas's deep laughter brought Fallon out of her trance, making her realize she'd spoken aloud.

"That's the nicest compliment I've ever received, especially since I don't think you had any intention of putting a voice to your thoughts."

Heated skin pressed against her back as Carson wrapped his arms around her, his large hands sliding south until the tips of his fingers brushed the top of her slit. Fallon's knees weakened as moisture flooded her sex.

"The way you respond to our touch is intoxicating,

Chef. The true magic of submission lies in recognizing your own power. Everything we do during a scene has one goal—pleasure. The only thing that trumps the priority of your happiness is your safety."

Fallon tried to focus on Carson's words, but when she felt the warmth of Silas's breath wash over the sensitive bare skin above her mons, all bets were off. The tip of his tongue speared between the wet lips of her labia, and Fallon's knees folded. She was grateful when Carson caught her easily, his chest vibrating with laughter against her back.

"Is Silas playing cat and mouse with your pearly clit, Chef? Tell me how it feels to have him pressing his mouth into your juicy pussy."

Is he kidding? I couldn't form a coherent sentence if my life depended on it. She managed a needy moan and felt a half-second of self-satisfaction she'd managed to make any sound at all.

"There's a sound every Dom loves to hear. Spread your legs wider for him, Chef. Give him access to all your sweet secrets, and I promise you won't regret it."

Regret? Oh no, indeed. Regret is the last thing on my mind. Questioning my sanity should probably be on my to-do list, but right now, I'm lost in a tsunami of pleasure, and everything else is fading into the background.

Silas was slow fucking her with his tongue, but it was the tip of his finger circling her rear hole that was melting her mind.

"Have you ever had anal sex, Fallon?"

She didn't immediately respond to Carson's inquiry, embarrassed to admit she'd always found the thought repulsive but damned if she wasn't rethinking her narrow view. The idea suddenly held a tremendous amount of appeal.

"Fallon, I asked you a question and expect an answer."

She'd read enough to know a simple shake of her head would not be enough, but when she opened her mouth to respond, the only sound that made it past her lips was a soft moan.

"While I enjoy hearing that sweet sound more than you can ever imagine, I need an answer to my question, Chef."

"N-N-No." Stuttering made her sound like the newbie she was, but it was all she could manage amid the on-slaught of sensation. When Silas pressed the tip of his finger against her rear hole, anything resembling control evapo-rated into a fine mist, and an orgasm she hadn't even known was on the horizon blasted through her like a freight train. Every cell in her body felt like it was on fire.

Scrambling for something to hold on to as the storm raged within, Fallon forgot she was supposed to hold her arms at her sides. Clutching the strong forearms wrapped beneath her breasts, she tried to ride out the storm. Colors so intense they defied description burst behind her closed eyes before vanishing into smoking swirls. When she finally opened her eyes, Fallon was surprised to find Silas standing so close, she could feel his body heat wrapping around her.

"I won't bother asking if you're interested in anal play—your body has already answered in a spectacular way. You taste sweeter than I'd imagined, and my expecta-tion was damned high. You'll be an addiction I'll never try to kick." Pressing his lips against hers, Silas did a slow exploration of her mouth.

Their kiss was spiked with her essence, giving Fallon the first taste of herself. The hint of tangy flavor ignited something deep inside her soul—a longing to explore, to finally find out what she'd been missing.

Chapter Ten

TOBI WAS ROOTED in place, listening as the man standing a few feet away talked on his phone. Whoever was on the other end of the call must have been demanding answers, Mr. Polished Loafers didn't have.

"I know you need the damned puzzle. Stop nagging. I've tracked her to Texas. The dumb bitch applied to get her license transferred here but only gave a general delivery address in Austin. Guess she plans to drop by the post office every day and pick up her sales flyers and clothing catalogs. Fucking hell, it's not like she has any friends or family who care enough to write her a damned letter. I made sure her coworkers didn't sound the alarm when she seemed to vanish into thin air." He paused long enough to cast a quick glance Lilly's way, but when she kept her focus on the bulletin board, he rolled his eyes and continued.

"She's supposed to be working as a fucking bartender in a kink club. How hard can she be to find? There can't be that many clubs in a state with more cows than people. Fucking hell, I didn't think I'd ever get to civilization."

There was a part of her that was half-insulted because he was completely ignoring her, but the sensible half knew better than to look a gift horse in the mouth. Setting her jaw, Tobi focused every ounce of her self-control on remaining in place. Damn, she wanted to step close enough to slap the arrogant bastard with enough force to send him ass over tea kettle into next week. When she'd heard him mention 'bartender at a kink club,' Tobi motioned Lilly to wait. They were returning from a shopping trip and had stopped outside Houston for fuel when Tobi overheard the man's comments and decided she needed to find out more. There were too many coincidences for him to be referring to anyone but Fallon Foster.

Lilly hadn't missed a beat, immediately understanding something was wrong. Tobi loved how in tune her mother-in-law was to everything happening around her. Lilly stayed where she was, but now, she was only pretending to read the colorful garage sale flyers taped to the wall. When Lilly slipped her hand into the large handbag slung over her shoulder, Tobi knew it was time for a distraction. There wasn't a chance in hill country hell the man would miss the weapon Lilly kept stashed in the stylish piece of luggage she called a purse.

One of Tobi's favorite Lilly memories was listening to her mother-in-law explain the differences between a purse and carry-on to airline employees when they questioned her at check-in. Lilly West was a former model whose successful career had allowed her the freedom to make substantial investments. She'd already been wealthy when she married oil men, Del and Dean West. It didn't matter that the three of them had built a diversified empire worth several billion; Lilly had no intention of paying a twenty-five dollars upcharge for a second carry-on.

When the jerk on the phone turned his attention to Lilly, Tobi saw something too close to suspicion flash in his eyes, so she did the only thing she could—she pretended to trip and fell against him. Not long after she'd married Kent and Kyle, they'd insisted she attend the self-defense classes they taught for the men and women joining their team of special operators. One of the sessions focused on ways to spot and avoid pickpockets. Tobi had become so proficient in lifting anything and everything from the trainees' pockets, the instructors still used her during their demonstrations. Kyle often laughed they'd wanted to make her safer, not train her for a new criminal career. When she and Lilly were safely back in their car, the other woman turned to Tobi and grinned.

"Did you get it?" Tobi gave the woman she considered her bonus mother a quick nod. "You are absolutely amazing, dear. Be sure to call the boys right away."

Tobi loved the way Lilly still referred to her grown sons as *the boys*. One of the things she loved the most about the family she'd married into was their unconditional love and the deep respect they had for one another.

Tobi didn't open the wallet—she'd made that mistake before. She'd gotten lectures from her husbands, their friends, and the local police about tampering with evidence more than once. She'd laughed when the officer lecturing her about the *chain of custody* suddenly realized she'd stolen the phone, now considered evidence. The mortified look on his face sent her into gales of hysterical laughter that further annoyed the jerk.

After disconnecting the call, Tobi grinned at Lilly.

"Kent seemed pleased, despite all his muttering about not being able to let us out of his sight for a hot minute without us getting into mischief. You know... the usual blah, blah, blah about being trouble magnets. Kyle's comments weren't as tactful, and I warned him calling his mother the Mistress of Mayhem would go over like a lead balloon. I probably shouldn't have warned him. It would have been fun to see you dress him down. Sometimes, he thinks he's all that and a bag of chips." She knew Kyle well enough to recognize his snark as a cover for concern, but it didn't give him permission to call her the Diva of Danger. Damn, damn, and double damn. She and Lilly hadn't been in the middle of anything interesting in months. Hell, they'd practically set a record for good behavior. Now that she thought about it, they were practically boring.

"Kyle said to tell you to drive safely, and he'll know if you're speeding." Tobi winced when Lilly's lips flattened, and her face turned an unattractive shade of crimson.

"Damn it, they put another tracker on my car, didn't they? I swear those two are going to need a proctologist to retrieve the next one." Swerving wildly across two lanes of traffic, Lilly took the next exit and pulled under a shade tree before releasing the truck latch and hopping out of the car. When she pulled what looked like a mini-metal detector from the trunk, Tobi started laughing.

"When did you get that?" Obviously, Lilly was tired of using the long-handled mirror she had the last time Tobi watched her look for one of the trackers her sons kept trying to hide in the frame of her car. Del and Dean West usually stood back, laughing at their sons' wasted efforts. The two men told Tobi they'd learned a long time ago the best way to handle their wife was to wait until she asked for their help—clearly, their sons still hadn't gotten the memo. A quick scan revealed two small magnetic trackers. After speaking briefly with a man leaning against his tractor-trailer rig, Lilly returned to the car.

"That ought to make them sit up and take notice. That truck is headed to Indiana. There are two race cars inside, and the driver said he'd be happy to slap the trackers on a couple of cars practicing on the speedway. I'll teach them to whine about my driving." Lilly put the car in gear and punched the gas, leaving enough rubber on the road to cut her new tires' life in half as they rocketed up the ramp and back onto the Interstate. "How long until they call? Shall we wager?"

"Hell, no. You mop the floor with me every time I'm dumb enough to bet with you. I swear I'm taking you to Vegas. Your luck is uncanny."

"It's not luck, dear. It's experience. When you're as old as I am, you'll be able to predict your children's behavior… oh, well, maybe I should edit that statement."

Tobi threw her head back and laughed. They both knew Tobi's daughter, Kodi, was anything but predictable. Kameron and Kodi were both academically gifted and had been in accelerated programs since starting school at three years of age, but that was where their similarities ended. Tobi and everyone else who knew him could predict what Kameron would do months in advance. Kodi, on the other hand, was wild as the wind, and no one knew from one moment to the next what she might say or do.

Kent and Kyle alternated between blaming their mother and their wife for their daughter's attitude, but everyone knew Kodi won the genetic lottery. She was a strategic planning master, often sitting in on her dad's mission meetings, offering insight way beyond her years. Kodi was secretly learning to fly—God only knew how she'd talked her grandfathers into helping her pull it off.

"I don't think they'll need to call since we have our phones. No matter how many times I get Kameron to hack the system and delete their access, they always figure it out." It was little more than an elaborate game of cat and mouse, but the bottom line was, she knew it was a safety issue and didn't actually want to be disconnected from them for more than an hour or two. That didn't mean she didn't enjoy giving them a run for their money once in a while for the sport of it.

"They can track your phone, but I brought a burner phone today just to annoy them. My sons have forgotten their mama doesn't take orders from them. Do you know they had the audacity to tell me it was time to trade in my convertible for something more appropriate for my age? Can you believe it?"

Tobi wasn't surprised Kent and Kyle wanted their mom to drive something safer. What shocked her was they'd had the nerve to say it out loud... to her! *Foolish men, they just guaranteed their mom is going to drive this pretty little Jag convertible until it falls apart.* Less than a minute later, Tobi's phone vibrated with an incoming message.

> **Kyle:** *Your phone is going one way, and mom's car is going another. I'm assuming there is a reasonable explanation.*

Tobi debated the best way to respond. He hadn't actually asked a question, so it was tempting to simply send back an okay emoji. She might have a valid argument when he complained later, but it would be impossible to keep a straight face when he asked if she had failed to hear the unspoken question.

> **Tobi:** *On our way home. ETA 30.* She was proud of herself. Damn, her diplomacy skills were on-point today.

> **Kent:** *Your phone is moving entirely too fast, Kitten. Tell the wild woman driving we're a hot second away from calling it in.*

Oh, hell no. She wasn't going to be used as the messenger girl between the three of them. She loved them all and followed Del and Dean's example anytime there was a conflict—they'd taught her the value of social distancing long before it was cliché. The two older men assured her silence was another hard-won lesson but well worth the effort. The past few years, Lilly and her sons had butted heads more frequently, and the trend had bothered Tobi until she'd read an article about role reversals as people age.

Smiling to herself, Tobi realized there was a silver lining she hadn't considered. The day was fast approaching when she'd be old enough to turn the tables and give Kodi and Kameron a run for their money. When she stopped to consider the challenges of parenting gifted twins, Tobi suddenly understood the joy radiating from her mother-in-law's stunningly beautiful face. Lilly must have sensed trouble brewing because she'd already slowed down before exiting onto the county road leading past her own house. Tobi laughed out loud when she saw Del and Dean sitting in their truck, waiting for their speed demon wife to fly by.

"They are too easy. I swear those sons of mine are the biggest tattletales in the world. For men whose entire lives have centered on keeping secrets and honoring confidences, they sure rat me out every chance they get. Those two have never met a bus they didn't want to throw me under." Waving at her husbands as they passed, Lilly giggled like a schoolgirl. "Damn, they are still hot. Since I was miles ahead of Tweedle Dee and Tweedle Dumb, I was driving safely, and I'll be appropriately rewarded. It's great to be me."

Tobi couldn't hold back her laughter. Lilly was an inspiration in so many ways. Their chance meeting led to Lilly making certain her sons granted Tobi the interview she hadn't been able to secure.

Still model gorgeous, Lilly West didn't care about her own or anyone else's outward appearance. She was too busy living her life to be tied up in what she called *shallow minutia*. By the time they drove through the gates leading to Prairie Winds, Tobi had ignored texts from both her husbands while assuring Gracie the world wasn't coming to an end, despite the hushed conversation her best friend overheard between her men.

"If Micah or Jax catch you lurking outside the control room, eavesdropping, you won't be able to sit for a week. Of course, that means we'll get to talk trash about them at the party for Fallon, so there is a bright side, I guess." Gracie let loose a string of Spanish curses making Tobi laugh out loud. "You better not be using talk-to-text. If they hear you call them bossy albinos with questionable parentage, you'll be lucky to attend the party."

When Gracie sent back a string of laughing emojis, Tobi knew one or both of her men had walked into the room. Her friend always reacted the same when Jax or Micah approached. The three of them were so perfectly suited, it was almost scary.

Two hours later, Tobi was still sitting in Kyle and Kent's office, answering the same questions for the third time, and finally had enough.

"Listen, I swear I have told you every word—complete with nuance, inflections, and accent—I overheard." Pointing to the wallet on Kyle's desk, she grinned. "I got you his name, address, and credit cards—what more could I have done?" Looking from Kent to Kyle, Tobi sighed. "You aren't mad because I lifted his wallet, are you?" Turning her attention to Silas, she shrugged. "It's baffling. They teach me a skill, then grumble when I use it." She knew the complaint was falling on deaf ears but was standing by her repeated claim that it was therapeutic to air the grievance. Silas chuckled as he shook his head.

"You're not pulling me into this, but for what it's worth, I've wondered more than once why they don't assign you to one of the teams. The only answer I've been able to come up with is they're afraid you and Jen McCall will take over."

"I knew there was a reason I liked you. You're brilliant."

"And you are incorrigible, but I want you to know how much Carson and I appreciate what you've done. You risked your own safety to help someone you barely know, which speaks volumes about who you are, Tobi. Even though those two,"—he nodded in Kent and Kyle's direction—"might not tell you often enough, they're proud of you as well."

Tears burn the back of her eyes. The sincerity of Silas's words made her chest feel tight, as if he'd reached in and squeezed her heart and touched her very soul.

He was dead-on about one thing; Kent and Kyle never held back their praise. While she and Gracie had been building their consulting business, they'd only offered their input and guidance when asked. When she and her best friend became discouraged, it had been their husbands who'd reminded them the path to success was never a straight line. The one time she'd been on the verge of quitting, it had been Kyle who'd reminded her small setbacks would provide the most valuable lessons.

"Thank you, Silas. Your words mean more than you know. One of the most important lessons I learned growing up in an abusive home was how important it is to protect others when you have the opportunity."

Shaking off the heaviness of the moment, Tobi grinned as her gaze moved to the glistening water of the pool outside the French doors overlooking the expansive backyard. The fading rays of a perfect Texas sunset danced over the surface. In the next few minutes, the underwater lights would turn on, tempting her to swim before driving home.

When they'd built a new house next door, the pool they'd added had been designed as an outdoor entertainment space. It was beautiful, but there was something magical about the pool at Prairie Winds. Maybe it was the memories—heaven only knew how many margarita parties they'd hosted since she'd married Kent and Kyle. Or maybe it was all the late-night heart-to-heart talks she had with friends, sipping wine while sitting on the edge. Whatever the reason, the pool behind what had once been her home was almost impossible to resist.

She'd been so lost in her thoughts, Tobi didn't realize Silas was no longer in the room until she felt Kent's arms wrap around tightly around her. Leaning her head against his chest, she let out a breath she hadn't realized she was holding.

"You never cease to amaze, sweetness. I know I speak for my brother as well when I say, I'm trying to decide whether to paddle your ass as a punishment for risking your safety or making the spanking a reward for seizing the opportunity and pulling off an incredible snatch and grab. Not only did you piece together who the man was talking about, you also made identifying him a slam dunk." Turning her away from the window, Tobi was surprised to find Kyle standing mere inches in front of her.

"Kitten, you are one of the bravest women I've ever met. Your heart is always in the right place, and no one could ever question your loyalty. The only thing missing is a sense of self-preservation. I swear to all things holy, my brother and I are going to have gray hair long before our time."

She wasn't sure where he was headed with this conversation, but she recognized the clanging bells of warning—from the sense of self-preservation he'd sworn she didn't have—reminding her of the value of silence.

Kyle was usually easy to read because he simply didn't believe in wasting energy playing word games or disguising his emotions. When she wanted to flirt and dance through the semantics tulips, Tobi sought out Kent. He was usually game for her occasional need to engage in a bit of verbal banter.

Damn, I haven't played stupid games for silly prizes in a while. No wonder I've been so restless.

"I swear someday we're going to keep her in the moment for an entire conversation." Kyle blew out a frustrated breath, the small tell one of his few outward signs of frustration.

This was the man she'd first met standing in the middle of a highway during what Texans referred to as a toad-strangler. She'd been desperate to get to a long-awaited meeting with Kent West, finally scoring the interview with his mother's help. It had been pure kismet the truck she finally flagged down was driven by Kent's twin brother Kyle.

A swat landed on her left ass cheek, generating more noise than heat, lifting her to her tiptoes and making her gasp in surprise. Early in their relationship, one of Tobi's biggest challenges was staying anchored in the here and now. Over the years, as her life filled with children and building a business, she flourished with laser-sharp focus.

Some part of her personality seemed to thrive amid chaos. Since she and Gracie stopped traveling and her kids were spending most of their time at their exclusive boarding school in Houston, Tobi found herself with more time on her hands. The more downtime she had, the worse her distraction became.

I need a damned hobby.

KYLE WATCHED TOBI worry her lip, her mind miles away— just as it had been on too many occasions the past few months. He and Kent agreed their requests for her to scale back her traveling had been ill-timed. It was painful to watch the woman who held their hearts struggle to find her footing. They'd considered taking turns traveling with her, but their own commitments didn't allow that luxury. The world was changing in ways no one dreamed possible just a few short years ago. He couldn't imagine letting Tobi and Gracie travel alone in a world drowning in chaos.

During their time in the Special Forces, he and Kent made their fair share of enemies. Since leaving the military, their contract work for Uncle Sam upped the stakes exponentially. Having a family made them vulnerable in ways they could never have imagined when they'd accepted the first mission. Finding Tobi in the midst of a blinding rainstorm, they'd immediately known she belonged to them, and letting her go had never been an option. Keeping the petite blonde whirlwind safe would always be their priority, but it was clear the two of them needed to rethink how it played out in her day-to-day life.

There had to be some way to balance Tobi's safety and happiness. Kyle vowed to find a solution that satisfied everyone's needs, but brainstorming would have to wait. Right now, there were other more pressing needs that needed to be met. Narrowing his focus to the woman who held his heart in the palm of her hand, Kyle gave a one-word command.

"Strip."

Chapter Eleven

S ILAS STOOD ON the balcony, staring out into the night. Looking down on the acreage between the club and the river was surreal because the area was never truly dark. The security lighting was seamlessly integrated with the landscaping, but with the flip of a switch, the whole damned place would burst into brilliance usually reserved for metropolitan runways. The scrape of a barefoot across the wood planks was all the warning he had before Carson leaned one hip against the rail and crossed his arms.

"You gonna tell me what that was about?"

Silas had expected the inquiry and hoped his friend left Fallon sleeping peacefully. They'd carried her upstairs after their playing behind the waterfall, then made love to her until they'd all collapsed in a tangle of limbs, sweat-damp, and smiling despite their exhaustion.

When their phones had both pinged with incoming messages a few minutes later, he and Carson flipped to see who was going to make their way downstairs. The hour he'd spent downstairs was damned unsettling. They'd only started establishing trust between the three of them, and now he was going to pull the rug out from under her. Damn. Why couldn't this be easy?

Giving Carson a quick run-down of what he'd learned, Silas watched concern, which mirrored his own, move across his friend's expression. There was always the chance she'd run—which meant they wouldn't be able to protect her, and getting her back safely wouldn't be easy. It was obvious she hadn't put much thought into covering her tracks.

She was scheduled to work behind the bar tonight at the club, but Kent and Kyle insisted Silas make the call after telling her what they'd learned this afternoon. He didn't know Fallon well enough to say for sure how she would react, but everything he'd learned led him to believe her work ethic would win—at least in the short term. She'd worked her way through college, no easy task, considering the astronomical cost of education.

"I don't think she'll leave until she talks to Lilly. It's just a hunch, but I can't see Fallon risking her relationship with her mother's friend."

Silas agreed with Carson's observation, but there was another way to look at the situation.

"What if she's worried about bringing trouble to Lilly and her family? Will her loyalty to friends prevent her from staying where we can keep her safe?" There wasn't any doubt in Silas's mind, Prairie Winds was the safest place for Fallon, but he was still concerned she hadn't been here long enough to understand how well trained the men and women were for this sort of thing. Their work for Uncle Sam was always under the radar and completely off the books, so the general public didn't know how skilled the team members were—both individually and as a unit.

"I'd appreciate being included in this conversation, but first, I want to thank you for your obvious concern for my safety. You're right... I am protective of those I care about, but I don't cut and run unless there's a damned good reason."

Silas wanted to kick himself for being so careless. How

could he be so unaware? Hell, he knew better than to stand with his back to an open door. Turning, he was relieved when she stepped forward to grasp his outstretched hand.

"You look hot in my shirt, Chef. I'd like it even better if it wasn't buttoned from top to bottom. Let's make an adjustment before we get into this discussion." Carson's effort to shift the tension was admirable, and the result was hotter than hell, but Silas wasn't sure it was entirely successful.

Fallon's expression was still set between disillusion-ment and a mulish determination to find out what had changed during her short nap. The evening breeze opened the placket of the Oxford shirt despite the two buttons Carson left fastened in the center. If they didn't get her inside, this conversation was going to be delayed, for heaven only knew how long.

"Let's take this inside before the moonlight waltzing down your bare breast short-circuits my brain, rendering me mute." Silas caught the twitch of her lips before leading her into the living room. When he started to pull her onto his lap, she shook her head and sat in a chair facing them.

"I want to be able to see you... both of you. I have a feeling this is going to be unpleasant, and I need to focus."

Silas hated the distance but understood her thinking.

"Let's hope it isn't as unpleasant as you're expecting. First of all, remember you are in the safest possible place." He didn't miss the way her spine straightened, her chin lifting in mock defiance. The subtle tell hadn't telegraphed the message she'd intended. Rather than signaling her desire to make her own decisions, she'd told him how worried she was everything was going to fall apart around her. She hadn't had time to develop the level of trust needed to know they would have her back. Hell, from what little he knew, Fallon had lost everyone important in her life. Trauma always takes a toll, and sometimes, the fallout is triggered by one final straw. Silas hoped he and Carson could act as the buffer she needed.

FALLON LISTENED AS Silas explained what Tobi overheard and tried to ignore the cold chill moving through her. Carson wrapped the throw from the back of the sofa around her shoulders; he must have seen the shiver she tried to hide.

"I don't understand why he would come all this way. It wasn't as if we had a grand affair or made any sort of commitment. He tried to paint me into a ménage corner with a damned teenager, for heaven's sake. Who does that sort of thing? He set it up so I'd walk in on them."

Fallon wasn't sure when she'd gotten out of her chair or how long she paced the length of the room before continuing.

"Damn it all to hell. Why does he give a rat's ass about my dad's puzzle?" Pausing, it suddenly occurred to her she'd never mentioned the gift to her asshat ex. "How did he know? About the puzzle, I mean. I told no one about it because the memory was too painful. That's why I haven't opened it. They were my dad's passion, not mine. I'm not sure I'd be able to solve the puzzle, and I'm not even sure I want to try. What's the point? It won't bring them back." She hated knowing she was teetering on the edge of losing it. The bubbling acid in her stomach always roared to life when she thought about all the unanswered questions about her parents.

"The company they'd always claimed to work for didn't even exist—at least not in any real sense. I tried to contact them after... the accident, but the number I had was to a switchboard. Their answers didn't make any sense." She'd gotten the strangest mental picture from a movie where the husband worked for the CIA and hid it from his wife by giving her a switchboard phone number.

"Is it possible they were agents of some kind?"

Silas's question was so dead-on she felt herself sag. How Carson closed the distance between them in time to keep her from collapsing to the floor was nothing short of a miracle.

"Let us help, Chef."

Carson's simple words were exactly what she needed to hear. It wasn't a command. He hadn't offered empty platitudes about sheltering her or given her any reason to believe he didn't think she was capable—he'd simply asked to help. Her heart skipped a beat, knowing it was time to take a leap of faith.

CARSON RECOGNIZED THE shift in Fallon's body language, signaling her willingness to let them help her face whatever lay ahead. A powerful wave of relief moved through him, knowing she was willing to take a chance on two men she'd known such a short time. He'd seen the knowledge in Silas's eyes that staying under the radar wasn't in her skill set. The truth was, it wasn't something most people ever considered, and making rushed decisions when strong emotions were in play didn't yield effective results.

He'd never worked a case when he couldn't track someone within days. One small sliver of information was all it took to blow a case wide open. Factoring in access to government and private security cameras, facial recognition software, and the ability to network worldwide with the push of a few buttons, the world suddenly became a very small place. It wasn't impossible to hide, but it took a tremendous amount of money and pre-planning to pull it off.

"Thank you. I promise you won't regret your decision. We'll do everything we can to ensure your safety. One of the first things I'd like to do is call Cameron Barnes. He's a friend and fellow club member. He's also a retired agent, or as retired as the intelligence community will allow. If your parents were a part of that world, Cam would know the details."

"If there's a puzzle involved, we'll ask Cam to bring along his friend and partner, Carl Phillips. Carl is a cryptologist, and I don't think a puzzle has been made, he doesn't love solving. Cam and Carl have a unique poly-relationship with Cam's wife and submissive, Dr. Cecelia Barnes."

"The pediatric surgeon?"

Carson shouldn't have been surprised Fallon had heard of CeCe; the woman was legendary in medical circles. At their nod, she let out a breath and flushed.

"Is this the doctor Ben was referring to, the doctor who is looking for a pharmacist? I didn't make the connection when it was mentioned earlier. I'd forgotten she had facilities in this area. Holy cats."

Carson grinned at her fan-girl moment. She was going to be surprised when she met CeCe—there wasn't a pretentious bone in the gifted doctor's body.

"So… Carl Phillips is good with puzzles, and he is partnered with a world-renowned surgeon and a not-so-former American version of 007. I feel like Alice… my world has turned upside down."

Carson leaned his head back and laughed. Fallon continued to surprise him at every turn.

"Wait." Fallon started pacing again, the shirt she wore doing little to hide her bare ivory flesh.

Damn, the woman was a fucking work of art. She needed to put back on the weight he suspected she'd lost during her cross-country travel. From what he'd seen, she had left with little, and knowing how hard she'd worked to pay for her education, he doubted she spent much on food.

At his core, Carson was a sexual dominant to the depths of his soul, and knowing she'd driven a piece-of-shit car from New York to Texas without spending money on food or a safe place to sleep made him want to pull her pert ass over his knee. Warming those lovely round ass cheeks might help her remember to take better care of herself in the future. Unfortunately, he nor Silas had earned that level of trust yet.

A sub had to be willing to place themselves in their Dom's hands for discipline or punishments to be effective. Without that relationship, the spanking wouldn't be anything other than a painful humiliation. The goal was to show her what she could gain in a D/s relationship, not what it would take from her.

"I'd like to talk to Lilly West tomorrow. She and my mom were friends. I've only met her a few times, but I sense she wouldn't be an easy woman to fool. If my parents were leading double lives, I suspect she knew or at least suspected. If she knew, I have to wonder if she is trying to protect me. I don't know... I need time to think... to sort this out."

Carson saw Silas's brow arch, the small shift in his expression the only outward indication Fallon had made a point neither of them had considered. Before he could say anything, she spun around. Facing them, he watched her entire body language shift.

"I think best when I'm busy. I'll be ready to go downstairs in half an hour."

"Kent and Kyle asked me to make the call about whether or not you work tonight." Silas deliberately paused, giving Fallon enough rope to make a mistake, but Carson saw the moment realization blossomed in her eyes. *Damn, I love smart women.* She didn't take the bait. Instead, she simply stood in silence and waited. "I told them it would be your decision, Fallon. I know you feel the electric pull arching between the three of us, so it's important for us to be completely transparent. I know I speak for Carson when I say we have no desire to control you. We only ask that you always consider your safety when making decisions."

This time, Fallon's body language shift was as obvious as it was welcome. Her shoulders relaxed, and she turned, so she fully faced them, a soft smile tilting the corners of her lips.

"Thank you. Knowing you aren't planning to micromanage my life is more important than you know. One of my ex-boyfriend's worst habits was the belief he was entitled to dictate my every move. In hindsight, I understand it for what it was, but it didn't start out that way." Waving her hand in the air as if it would erase the bad memory, she shook her head. "I'm not going to get into that now. Life is too short to focus on things we can't change. I now recognize the early signs of emotional abuse and know how to avoid it."

Carson started to respond, but something about her body language made him hold back. Fallon was winding herself up, and he wasn't sure why. His grandmother always swore women pulled energy from those around her. He'd talked to her about a girlfriend who was acting strange, and she told him to look at his own actions for the answer. It hadn't taken him long to understand what the older woman had been trying to tell him. Gray eyes, so much like his own, had glittered with satisfaction. His grandmother was cagey. She'd made little effort to hide her dislike of the girl Carson brought home several times during his sophomore year. It was humbling to admit the Scott matriarch had been right. The woman he'd been dating was a gold digger and as phony as a three-dollar bill. A decade later, Carson was mature enough to admit he'd been led around by his dick and was grateful he'd finally seen the light.

"While you're getting ready for work, we'll set up a time for you to talk with Lilly. You'll probably want to sleep in after working late, so we'll see if she'd be interested in a late lunch. The woman loves to entertain, so we'll make certain one of us is available to drive you." Silas grinned when her mouth flattened. Shaking his head, he added, "Your car hasn't been fixed yet, sweetheart. I won't bother repeating what the Wests had to say about the state of your transportation. If you have an issue with how they're dealing with it, talk to them."

"I will do just that. I can't afford to put a bunch of money into a car. A fancy car is not something I care much about. I'd rather invest in a business or home. My car needs only get me from point A to point B."

"Safely." Carson couldn't hold back the addition. She didn't argue with his small caveat, giving a sharp nod without responding before walking from the room. He let out a slow breath and grinned at Silas. "I'd pay big bucks for that ticket. Watching her argue with Kent and Kyle about her car would be damned entertaining. Throwing their bossy asses under the bus was an inspired decision."

"It's only fair since they sent it to the crusher. It will be fun to watch them battle with her. They've had it too easy with Tobi and Lilly lately. I swear the subs at the club have become borderline predictable and boring."

Carson threw his head back and laughed.

"You've done it now. Didn't your New Age community teach you about the dangers of speaking intentions out loud?" Looking out the window, Carson grinned. "And a full moon to boot. Damn. Make sure you let the Doms know this is on you, not me. Call Lilly. I'm going to see if Cooper has a way to contact Cam. I hate to pull him into the middle of this, but if anyone can get an emergency message thru, it's Hicks."

"He and Catalina are on the other side of the damned planet on a special assignment. No one, not even her brother, knows how to contact them." If Austin Adler couldn't get to his sister, there wasn't anything to do but wait.

Silas was usually a patient man, but in this case, nervous pinpricks of awareness and dread were making him antsy. He'd already asked Micah Drake to find out everything he could about Hagan Brody. The little he knew didn't add up. In Silas's experience, when a man's interest in kink met rejection, it was easier to walk away than pursue a woman who wasn't interested. He'd have never chased one across the country.

If Brody was willing to pursue Fallon, there had to be another reason, and Silas needed to find out what it was.

Chapter Twelve

F ALLON HAD FORGOTTEN what hard work bartending was—damn, her feet hurt. Her back ached from carrying freaking bottles of water from the back storeroom. Everything ached, but she was happier than she'd been in over a year. The staff she worked with were friendly. They'd answered her questions and helped her master the identification system that assured members didn't participate in scenes after drinking anything with alcohol.

One piece of protocol had been easy for her to remember—addressing the Dominants as Sir and Ma'am. It was a point of etiquette her parents had always insisted on, so the habit was already deeply ingrained. Hearing subs refer to their play partners, spouses, and Dominants as Master seemed odd, and she hoped to get past thinking it was degrading. Aside from anything involving body fluids, the only other aspect of the lifestyle she'd read about that totally repulsed her was humiliation. For the life of her, Fallon couldn't understand why anyone would willingly submit themselves to some things she'd read about.

"Hey, girl, how did your first shift go? We didn't scare you off yet, did we?" Tobi bounced up onto a bar stool, flashing a huge grin and pulling Fallon out of her thoughts.

"It was fun, but I'm humbled to find out how out of shape I am. Holy Helga, who knew those cases of water were so heavy?" The bar where she'd worked during college had been paranoid as hell about injuries, so she'd been required to use a handcart to move anything heavier than a six-pack of beer. Once she'd started at the pharmacy, she'd worked such strange hours, it became difficult to establish a workout routine, and the gym in her small apartment complex was overrun with creeps.

"You are supposed to have one of the male subs bring the cases up for you. Didn't they tell you?"

"Yes, but I never seemed to know I needed help until it was too late to track someone down."

"Chef, that excuse isn't going to cut it." Carson's arm snaked around her from the back, and with a quick tug, she was surrounded by his warmth.

Closing her eyes just for a second, Fallon absorbed his warmth and strength, hoping no one heard the small whimper she hadn't been able to hold back. When she opened her eyes, Tobi was grinning like a Cheshire cat.

"Oh, this is wonderful. Master Carson and Master Silas had almost given up finding you." Kyle and Kent quickly flanked their wife, giving Fallon the impression they hoped to keep her from talking herself into trouble. "And then to think they smacked you with a mirror. Damn, what an introduction. At least Master Kyle didn't run over me on the highway."

"It was a near miss, and you know it, Kitten. I'd never have forgiven myself if I hurt you." Kyle's tone reflected a sincerity and softness Fallon hadn't expected.

It seemed the club members she'd overheard talking about Kyle West considered him the harder of the two men. She knew they were considered mirror-image twins, but she was pleased to find it hadn't been difficult for her to tell them apart. Their different personalities made the distinction clearer, and she wondered if they could switch the personas at will like she'd seen other twins do so often.

"But you didn't hit me, so I'm not sure I see your point. On the other hand, Fallon was sent ass over tea kettle into the ditch." Turning her attention back to Fallon, the bubbly blonde grinned. "You did a great job covering up the bruises, Fallon. I was going to offer to help, but… well, I got distracted by two very handsome men this afternoon." She leaned against Kyle, making him chuckle.

"She took a nap after our water sports. Shameless." He nodded toward Silas, who was making his way across the main room. "Mom tells me the two of you are going to chat tomorrow. She wants the meeting to take place at my parents' home. The property is directly adjacent to Prairie Winds but doesn't have the same level of security."

Fallon recognized the deliberate pause for what it was, but if he thought she was going to let him off the hook without a full explanation, he didn't give her enough credit. A fleeting smile or resignation was the only outward acknowledgment he knew she was onto him.

"In the interest of security, I've asked her to host you on-site. You'll have lunch in the gazebo, so you'll have privacy."

Fallon didn't miss the subtle shift in Tobi's posture. Something her husband said didn't sit well with the other woman, and Fallon made a mental note to find out what had triggered her response.

"After you talk to our mother, Kent and I would like to speak with you. Carson and Silas are welcome to join the conversation, and I hope they do. Communication is always key when you are working to keep someone safe."

Fallon had to give the man credit—he was a master at spinning an understatement. She might not be the most experienced or worldly woman around, but she'd worked in bars long enough to spot a smokescreen at a thousand paces.

"I appreciate your concern, but I'm curious about something." He blinked in surprise, making her want to smile. Kyle West wasn't a man accustomed to being questioned. If Fallon was guessing, she'd put good money on him allowing only two women to push him away from the hardline he seemed to take with those around him. "You mentioned the security being less at your parents, which implies you don't have the entire property covered with cameras and audio-recording equipment."

Kyle's lips quirked a second before a broad smile spread over his face.

"Jigs up, brother. Level with the woman so we can all get to sleep. She's going to find out anyway, and you can save us time and entertainment at your expense when she leads you by the nose to the inevitable reveal." Kent West shook his head, amusement making his eyes sparkle. Redirecting his attention to Fallon, she watched him turn on the charm and wanted to laugh.

Hello. Bartender in a college bar for over six years. Hell, I worked for two years with a fake ID. I wasn't even old enough to drink when I started. Thinking I'd miss this ploy is borderline insulting.

"I swear I've tried to civilize him, Fallon. Unfortunately, nothing seems to stick. He regularly underestimates women—particularly those he believes require his protection."

Oh, brother. Kent West was laying it on thick and smooth. It seemed Kyle wasn't the only one who underestimated her. Fallon crossed her arms over her chest, leveling a look at him she hoped he understood.

"We are all tired. How about I help you cut to the chase. I've dealt with enough drunken frat boys to know a snow job when my nose is being rubbed in it." Tobi snickered and gave her a discreet thumbs-up. "I don't have any illusions about privacy during my meeting with your mother. I only ask that we aren't interrupted. I want to ask questions and listen to her responses without worrying about what everyone around me is thinking. Focusing on what your mother knows will help me put together the pieces. I may not be a cryptologist like your friend, Carl Phillips, but I know my dad wouldn't have given me a puzzle I had no hope solving." All three Wests reacted to her mention of Carl Phillips—interesting.

"Our team will monitor visually, but we won't eaves-drop on your conversation. You need to be able to ask questions, confident my mother can respond candidly. I assure you she has already torn several large patches off my hide during our earlier... negotiation."

"Juicy deets to follow. I can hardly wait for the party version of this conversation, but I'm sacked. Let Fallon get some sleep; she'll need it to keep up with Lilly. I love that woman to death, but she is a firecracker, and it's in your best to stay alert."

Fallon sagged back against Carson without realizing how tense she'd become. Grateful for Tobi's intersession, Fallon turned to Silas, giving him a small smile.

"Tobi's right. I haven't spent a lot of time with Lilly, but it doesn't take long to know I need to be in top form to find out everything I'd want to know. My mom counted Lilly among her oldest and dearest friends, so it may be tough to crack through that loyalty." Carson's arms tightened around her, infusing her with strength. "I'll be happy to share whatever information I learn. The more we know, the sooner this can be resolved. I'm not thrilled about having the rug yanked out from under me by the controlling jackass who wanted me to share a bed with a teenager."

Fallon felt the rage she'd been working so hard to suppress, boiling its way to the surface. She'd spent the entire evening mulling over everything she'd experienced since her parents' death. The more she thought about it, the stranger things seemed. Hagan's obsession with her always seemed too good to be true, and she'd wondered more times than she cared to remember, thinking there was a catch. There'd been warning flags, but she'd been focused on starting her career at the expense of common sense.

"Brody's loss is our gain. I'm sorry for the pain he's caused, but we fully intend to kiss every square inch of you and make it all better." Carson's whispered words against the shell of her ear had their desired effect.

Warmth ebbed slowly through her, pushing the anger out of her mind and replacing it with a gentle wave of desire. The group agreed to meet again after Fallon's lunch with Lilly before moving in separate directions.

Fallon smiled at the cleaning crew coming through the back door. Her coworkers had assured her there was no reason to do her own clean-up behind the bar, and Fallon had been grateful to hear the news. Clean up after the bar closed had always been her least favorite part of the job. She's been busy enough all evening, she hadn't been able to keep up beyond doing the bare minimum.

"Don't worry, being hired for this job is a plum gig. One of our members owns the company, and the Club underwrites a membership for any of the employees assigned to the club. Trust me, they are thrilled to be here." Carson's soft laughter caught the attention of one of the crew members, who gave him a friendly wave.

"Hi, Master Carson. Thanks for the suggestion for my research project. The professor was impressed, and I was the first applicant approved." The young man's face practically glowed with pride, happiness radiating around him.

"Happy to help. I'm glad it worked out. Remember to touch base with my office about an internship. My executive assistant has your letter of recommendation, so you need to stop by and pick it before your interview. Give her a heads up, and she'll arrange a tour. I know you have a lot on your agenda, but the slots will fill quickly."

Fallon lost track of how many times the young man nodded and thanked Carson before the three of them were out of earshot.

"A letter of recommendation? Damn. Either Brooks Wilson is a long-lost brother, or he's fucking brilliant."

Fallon was suddenly interested as well. Carson hadn't struck her as being over salacious with praise. She'd heard him described as one of the toughest Doms during the required training course and inwardly cringed at a few of the stories she'd heard about his creative punishments.

"The kid's gift is uncanny. I've never met anyone like him. If I don't get him signed, Phoenix Morgan will lure him to Montana." Carson didn't offer any further explanation, leaving Fallon to assume Phoenix Morgan was a competitor.

She didn't have a large network of close friends in New York. Her parents hadn't socialized a great deal because they'd traveled extensively for work, and Fallon had spent her free time studying and working. A cloud of melancholy crowded around her as she wondered what she'd missed by living in a city where looking someone in the eye was considered a challenge, so you learned early to keep your head down.

"What triggered your sudden mood shift, sweetheart?"

Fallon was surprised to find the elevator had already delivered them to the top-floor apartment, and Silas was holding the door open, waiting for her to step through. She'd been so lost in thought, everything around her had faded to the background.

"Who or what is Phoenix Morgan? A competitor? A friend? Old flame?" Damn, why has she added that last part? She didn't have any right to ask any of those questions, and the last one made her look like a jealous twit.

Carson blinked in surprise, then grinned.

"Phoenix Morgan writes the best gaming software in the world. He started in high school. Scary smart and recruits the best of the best from around the world, hustling them to his lair in Montana. We're friends and have teamed up a time or two on projects, but I swear if he snatches another intern out from under me, I'm going to sic his equally talented but much nicer wife on his tail."

"Fallon, our work and lifestyle offer us a lot of reasons to travel and network with people who share our interests. You haven't had those opportunities yet, but I promise they'll come faster than you can imagine."

She took Silas's outstretched hand and stepped out of the elevator.

"I'm sorry, I know I don't have a right to ask questions. Fatigue tends to blow my social filters out of the water." She was rarely this outspoken. One of the hazards of having been raised without siblings was an ultra-fine social filter. The Thumper Rule was drilled in so deep, the only time Fallon let her guard down enough to say something rude or out of line was when she was exhausted or drinking. She could control one situation by not imbibing, but the other gave her trouble more often than she wanted to think about.

"Sure you do. We've told you what we want from you. What we failed to do was tell you what you could expect from us." Carson smoothed the backs of his fingers along the underside of her jaw, his pupils dilating when she felt herself leaning into the touch. "We can't change our past, Chef, but we'll do everything we can to make sure it never blindsides you. We'll be as open as we can be and honest to a fault."

"It's also important for you to know, we only share with each other. We'll never bring anyone else into our bed."

She appreciated their candor and assurance. Hagan had never made a promise of fidelity, and she hadn't asked for one, so in some ways, perhaps she'd set herself up to fail. On the long drive to Texas, Fallon promised to avoid entanglements. She'd wanted to get her license, find a job and apartment, then move on with her life. Good heavens, fate loved to listen to her requests then do as it damned well pleased.

"I'd never cheat, either. It's degrading to everyone involved. My mother once told me the greatest gift my dad had ever given her was his loyalty. I have never forgotten the sincerity in her voice. I'd known then, cheating would always be a deal-breaker for me."

"Perfect. The Universe never makes a mistake, Fallon. It will fight tooth and nail to get you where you need to go. The plan may look random to us—perhaps even questionable—but it's not. Often, the best gifts are preceded by the most difficult loss."

Fallon wasn't sure she agreed that catching her boy-friend in bed with a teenager qualified as a difficult loss. She'd been pissed rather than hurt by his action.

"No, sweetheart. I can see by your expression you've missed my point. Losing your parents set this in motion."

Fallon couldn't argue his point, although the coffee date she'd had with her dad seemed to be the point where her life began careening out of control. Maybe the puzzle would yield an answer. She should have tried to solve it after their funeral, but she'd been so lost in a fog of grief, the only way she'd known to survive the pain was throwing herself into her work.

The shirt she'd worn while working slipped from her shoulders, the sensual slide of soft cotton bringing her back to the moment.

"Everything else can wait. Nothing matters at this moment but making certain you know you are ours. You are perfect for us. It may seem sudden to you, but we've been waiting for you. Honestly, we'd almost given up finding a woman we both believed capable of handling us. You, Chef, are more than capable." Carson was pressing kisses along the top of her shoulder, sending goosebumps skittering down her arm. "So responsive. Fuck me, I want to taste every inch of you."

Fallon gasped when he picked her up and started down the hall. She hadn't been expecting the sudden shift in position and giggled when she realized they were all but sprinting toward the bedroom.

"Did I miss a fire alarm?" Fallon cocked her head to the side, pretending to listen for a screeching alarm when Carson finally set her back on her feet.

"Indeed, you did, sweetheart. We've watched you

work all evening without interfering. Damned hard to do when all we wanted was to pull you into the backroom and ravage you." Silas knelt in front of her, pulling off her shoes. The relief was immediate, and she moaned in appreciation. "You'll get a nice long foot rub while you soak in the tub."

A bath and foot massage sounded heavenly, but those temptations weren't lighting up every cell in her suddenly highly aroused body. Silas finished stripping her, then handed her off to Carson. Damn, how had he undressed so quickly?

Chapter Thirteen

W<small>ATCHING</small> C<small>ARSON</small> <small>LEAD</small> Fallon into the bathroom made him pause his frantic striptease. Damn, she was stunning and completely unaware of the effect she had on everyone she came into contact with. He and Carson stood aside all night, watching and wondering how anyone so perfect stayed single for so long. *Fate.* It was the only explanation.

Her radiant smile lit up the entire bar, drawing people in without making the slightest effort. He'd never seen so many people linger around the bar. Ordinarily, the Doms were more than happy to send one of the club's trainees for whatever they needed. Tonight Doms and subs alike seemed to make the bar the center of attention. Their reaction wasn't difficult to understand. Fallon radiated positive energy. There was a certain mystical vibration moving around her others might not understand, but Silas's background was different. He recognized energy shifts in people before anyone else detected a problem. Hell, it was one of the reasons he'd been so successful in security work. Being able to predict someone's behavior in advance gave him an enormous advantage.

It had only taken him one look to recognize her as theirs. She'd looked up, and the world shifted on its axis—equal parts gut-punch and relief. Now, watching her pert ass walk from the room, he sent up a silent prayer of thanks for the chance to make her theirs. Keeping her safe was their first concern. He hoped like hell Lilly West could shine a light on Fallon's parents' background. Hagan Brody had mentioned the puzzle, but none of them wanted to solve it until Carl returned. Maybe they were being paranoid, but that damned Tom Hanks movie where a wrong answer destroyed the contents kept playing in his head.

Whatever Fallon's dad slipped inside the cylinder had been important, or he wouldn't have made certain she had it. The timing was too perfect, and Silas didn't believe in coincidences. *The Universe never takes a chance, son.* His mother's often-repeated words moved through his mind as he finished undressing.

Making his way into the bathroom, Silas was grateful he'd taken the time to come upstairs a few minutes ago to set up everything. A silver platter of fruit and cheese, surrounded by crackers and pieces of French bread, sat on a low table beside the sunken tub. Bubbles almost a foot high when he left had barely settled despite Fallon lying back against the edge.

Carson had piled her hair atop her head in some sort of fancy twist he'd done a hundred times before. The man had a family filled with women and claimed they'd all made him help them with their hair. Silas assumed the story was wishful thinking on his friend's part until he'd spent a holiday with the rowdy crew and seen the ladies lined up for one of Cousin Carson's fancy *dos*. It had been the damnedest thing Silas had ever seen.

Silas slipped into the tub, settling close enough to pull her feet into his lap. Stroking his thumbs along the arched curve of her foot, Silas smiled at her soft moan of pleasure.

"Oh, my stars and summer gardens. I swear your hands

are pure magic." The melodic tone of her voice and interesting phrasing made Carson chuckle against her back.

"Chef, if you think Silas's hands are magic on your feet, you're in for a real treat when he pushes them deep into your heat. He'll stroke them over your G-spot, launching you over the moon and into a space so drenched in pleasure, you'll be convinced you'll never be the same." Silas watched the blush of arousal bloom over her heart, then slowly ebb its way up until her cheeks practically glowed.

"The rules for tonight are simple. Relax. Feel. Enjoy." Silas and Carson knew she was exhausted, but she was also strung too tight to sleep.

He'd been damned proud of how she'd handled the conversation with Kyle West and knew Carson felt the same way. It took most people several encounters with Kyle to understand his communication style—Fallon had seen through his smokescreen immediately. She'd been patient and polite but hadn't taken the bait when he'd tried to lead the conversation. The look of admiration in Tobi's eyes was impossible to miss, and Silas was pleased to know her new friend knew exactly when to interject herself into the conversation.

"That's right, Chef. Let us show you the sweet benefits and perks of having two men focused on your pleasure."

Tonight had been torture. Silas and Carson had stopped by the bar a few times to check on her, but most of their evening had been consumed with their normal duties as Dungeon Monitors. One of the club's newest members seemed to think Carson should spend the entire evening entertaining her. He and Silas played with the woman once, and she'd read more into the scene than they intended. Weeks later, she was still obsessed. When Silas asked if they had any connection outside the club, Carson had rolled his eyes.

Carson Scott might refer to himself as an internet jockey, but his resume was damned impressive—not as notable as his bank balance, but still worthy. Coming from a family whose work ethic far exceeded their ability to turn their efforts into cash, Carson took the lessons and left the swamps of East Texas as soon as he could convince a college admittance board he could handle the workload. Acing all their tests before he was old enough to drive caught the attention of one of the college scholarship committee members.

Dell West was so impressed with Carson's taped interview, he'd anonymously funded the young man's education. Dean and Dell signed Carson as a contract employee before he'd decided a diploma wasn't worth the time spent listening to professors droll on about outdated technologies and politics. When he'd argued Dean and Dell should wait to see where he found employment, they'd explained all the reasons he should be independent. Over the years, Carson heard about other instances where the elder Wests quietly helped people become successful. He and Silas vowed to do the same and were looking forward to reaching the point where those opportunities presented themselves.

"We're from neighboring boroughs. Her family has an over-inflated sense of power and confuses forced compliance with adoration."

Carson's response to his inquiry about Nancy Dressler prompted more questions than it answered, but at the time, Silas hadn't seen a reason to push his friend for an explanation. After this evening, Silas was more than interested. All evening, the woman had pursued Carson relentlessly despite being told no. When Carson refused to explain, Nancy changed tactics.

Standing to the side of the club's cavernous main room, she'd simply watched. Silas had to give her credit; she was shrewd. She'd quickly locked in on Carson's interest in Fallon. Her eyes narrowed, and Silas felt as though a cold wind had blown through the damned room. Watching the play of emotions on Nancy's face, Silas could almost hear her mind spinning with possibilities, and the crease in her brow gave him the distinct impression it would not bode well for Fallon. Making a mental note to discuss the issue with Carson, Silas focused on the woman sitting in front of him.

"Seeing you surrounded by bubbles is a delight, sweetheart." The soapy froth was quickly diminishing, revealing her taut, pink nipples. Silas was eager to see how much pressure it would take for Fallon to come from nipple clamps. Damn, she was going to look amazing in silver and turquoise.

"Your talented hands are wasted working security." Silas nodded his thanks; her compliment assured him she was enjoying his touch. "When I was in college, I usually walked to work. It wasn't far, but the walk home after my shift at the bar was brutal."

"You walked home after work? Alone?"

Silas smiled to himself, knowing Fallon wasn't just pressing one of Carson's hot buttons—she was jumping up and down on the entire keypad with both feet.

"Driving didn't make sense since I would have had to park so far away, it was actually safer to walk from home. Parking garages in college towns are dangerous. The one I would have had to use was almost the same distance as my apartment, and the neighborhood was nuts." Fallon must have sensed the tension running through Carson. As a born and bred southern boy, Carson's need to protect the women in his life was second nature. Add in his sexually dominant personality, and you had a man guaranteed to make their New York subbie crazy.

"Your boss was okay with that arrangement?" Carson's jaw was set, and he was speaking through clenched teeth.

Silas understood the other man's frustration, but he felt like his friend was beating a dead horse.

"It wasn't my boss's decision, Carson. I know you think I was being careless, but you're wrong. After I lost my parents, I was more safety conscious than I'd ever been. Yes, I know it was an accident, but that didn't stop the niggling feeling something wasn't right."

"Always listen to your gut, sweetheart. Instinct is rarely wrong." Silas and Carson would keep a very close eye on her until they were convinced she was no longer in danger. Until they knew what was inside that damned puzzle, it was going to be difficult to let her out of their sight.

Skimming the tips of his fingers up the inside of her leg, Silas was pleased to see her eyes widen as her pupils closed in on the outer ring of color. Within minutes, the three of them were climbing into the mammoth bed the Wests commissioned when they first built the apartment over the club. They'd always planned to share a wife and had left the master suite empty until she made her way into their lives.

"You know what we want, Chef. If you have any reservations, now is the time to voice them. Your safe word will always work, but it will end play until the next day. Use the word yellow if you feel uncertain. That gives us the chance to take a break and address your concerns. We looked over your club information, and everything we've planned for you aligns perfectly with your interests."

Her shudder was perfect.

FALLON WAS WORRIED Silas and Carson were going to talk her into a coma. Whoever started the rumor about women being the chatty ones obviously hadn't spent any time with Carson and Silas. Gawdy garters, she wanted to tell them to get on with it or be quiet so she could sleep. Fucking hell, she was standing naked in a bedroom clearly designed for sex, and Carson and Silas suddenly turned into Dr. Phil and Jerry Springer.

When Silas leaned his head back and laughed, Fallon wished the floor would open up and swallow her. She wasn't sure how much she spoke aloud, but any of the thoughts would have been too much. Damn. Damn. Damn.

"Ordinarily, we won't be so accommodating, but in this case, I'm willing to admit you are right. We've been chatting when we should have been playing." Silas's eyes danced with amusement. "Did you wear your plug as instructed?"

Fallon felt her face heat with embarrassment. Holy crap on a cactus, did they have to be so blunt?

"Yes. It's in my locker downstairs." It had taken her forever to clean the blasted thing. As it turned out, the locker room was akin to Grand Central Station. The other submissives were probably past the embarrassment of using the special sink the club provided for washing toys, but she'd been too uncomfortable to clean the toy until one of the brief moments when the locker room was empty.

"Perfect. Come here." Taking her hand, Silas led her to the small seating area. The first thing she noticed was the soft throw usually folded on the end of a small sofa was spread over the seat of a silk upholstered chair. She'd noticed the chair earlier—the simple design and lack of armrests made her wonder why the Wests included an uncomfortable piece of furniture in the limited space. She was surprised when Carson stopped in front of the covered seat and pulled her to stand facing him.

"This chair was specifically designed for ménage, Chef. We've already ordered a couple for our home." Fallon's surprise must have shown in her expression, making Carson grin. "It may not look comfortable, but I assure you, in a few minutes, it will be your favorite piece of furniture." Before she could ask any of the questions racing through her mind Carson sealed his lips over hers, sending white-hot need racing up and down her spine.

Mini bolts of lightning opened the floodgates in her sex. Her cream flowed freely, making her channel slick before pushing further to coat the petals of her labia. Somewhere in the very back of her mind, Fallon hoped they wouldn't notice the slickness she worried would trickle down the inside of her thigh. *Nothing like making yourself look like a wanton hussy.* Fallon pushed aside the self-conscious thoughts. There would be plenty of time to judge her behavior later... a lot later.

Carson's kiss was melting her mind. His tongue traced the ridges lining the roof of her mouth before exploring every inch. The sensual caress of his tongue warmed her lower lip before he pulled back. His gaze was filled with heated desire she swore had a magnetic effect. Before she could stop herself, Fallon leaned close enough to feel the warmth of his breath brush against her forehead.

"Damn, Chef, you are tempting me in ways no other woman ever has." Carson's admission must have amused Silas—his soft chuckle vibrated against her back. He turned her to face him, his eyes filled with desire.

"Carson is never tempted to stray from the script, sweetheart."

"I've never kissed a woman I considered mine. The difference is astonishing."

Carson's hands settled around her waist, the heat making her skin feel alive in a way she'd never imagined possible. Silas framed her face with his large hands, tilted her head to the perfect angle, and pressed his lips to hers. His kiss was slower but no less intense. By the time he finally pulled back, she realized her knees had folded out from under her.

"You melted me." The words were barely audible, but Fallon felt a small sense of pride, knowing she had enough functioning brain cells to speak. Silas smiled as he held her until she was able to stand on her own.

"We have only started. Let us show you why this chair is a club favorite."

Chapter Fourteen

FALLON PULLED IN gasping breaths, her heart pounding so hard she wondered if her ribs would shatter. "Best piece of furniture ever." Fallon's sense of pride she'd been able to speak was out of proportion to the simple statement she managed around the dense fog clouding her brain. As soon as Fallon saw Carson leaning back in the chair, she'd understood the appeal. Being able to lower herself onto his erection, taking him into her body at a pace she could control, was empowering.

He would carry the half-moon imprints of her fingernails for several hours, and Fallon sent up a silent prayer of thanks she hadn't broken the skin. Nothing screamed a lack of sophistication and experience like poking holes in your partner. Her first release blindsided her before he was fully seated inside her channel. The smile Carson gave her held equal parts pride and warning. They hadn't specifically told her to hold off her orgasm, but she'd read enough to know it was an implied expectation.

"Don't worry, sweetheart. Your reaction was damned amazing to watch, and from the tortured look on Carson's face, I'd say it was intense for him as well. There will be plenty of time for play rules. Absent instructions, follow your body's lead. We've been Doms for a long time, so we'll know when you are close to release."

Each subsequent orgasm had been more intense than

the one before. By the time Silas eased himself into her rear hole, Fallon was convinced she was being split in two. How her body accommodated both men was a mystery for the ages, but the intensity of pleasure quickly collapsed all the synapses of her nervous system. All the cells had been firing like Revolutionary War cannons, but none of the messages hit their target. Hell, after living in a fog of grief and exhaustion for so long, Fallon hadn't thought it was possible to lose herself so completely in pleasure.

"Stay where you are, Sweetheart. I'll be right back." Silas gave the command as he pulled from her body. The feeling of his cock retreating had her gasping before a soft moan passed her lips. Both men chuckled, but neither said anything. Carson's arm fell over her waist, anchoring her to his chest. Fallon would have laughed at his attempt to keep her from falling when it seemed he barely dropped his arm over her but doubted he'd find the observation amusing.

"She's not going anywhere and has earned herself a couple of swats for doubting I can keep her from tumbling to the floor. Insulting as hell."

Fallon might have been concerned if she hadn't felt his chest vibrating against her cheek with silent laughter.

"I didn't say any such thing. There has to be a loophole for inference and erroneous interpretation."

"Darlin', I was born and raised in the swamps by women who taught me, listening involves more than what your ears hear. You have to listen with your soul if you want to know what someone is thinking."

Damn. Fallon couldn't think of a response since she had no experience with the culture of southern women. She'd heard they were fiercely loyal, with mystical gifts sometimes bordering on spooky, but she'd yet to meet anyone outside the tightknit Prairie Winds Club circle.

"We'll make sure you are well-prepared to meet Carson's family. Mine, on the other hand, will be a breeze."

Fallon yelped when she realized Silas was standing directly behind her. She tried to recover a small shred of decency by closing her splayed legs, but a stinging swat stopped her.

"Never hide yourself from us, Fallon. There is no room for embarrassment in the relationship we want with you." She started to protest, but another swat on the opposite side made her clamp her mouth shut. Silas used a warm, wet cloth to clean her most intimate parts. Despite her earlier attempts to forestall him, Fallon finally relaxed in his care.

"That's better, Chef. Let us take care of you. We're looking forward to showing you there are a lot of hidden perks to a D/s relationship."

Carson's words vibrated against her chest, sinking deep into her soul. It surprised her to realize, for the first time since she left New York, she'd pushed all her worries to the back burner. She hadn't worried about Hagan or what that blasted puzzle might reveal. She lost herself in the pleasure with no concern for the snag she'd hit getting her license transferred. Fallon might be physically exhausted from her first ménage experience, but there was a new level of energy simmering below the surface she'd never experienced.

CARSON COULD PRACTICALLY hear the wheels of Fallon's mind spinning as she tried to sort through her emotional response to ménage. He'd felt the intensity of their connection, and his feelings were reflected in her eyes. Over the years, he'd seen subs completely shut down after a scene as emotionally charged as the one they'd shared. It felt like they'd waited an eternity for her, giving Carson and Silas more than enough time to plan for every contingency, including this one. But like all plans you are forced to make based on vague details, everything starts getting dicey when reality hits.

Once Silas finished patting Fallon's tender tissues dry, he lifted her from Carson's chest. When she swayed on her feet, Silas didn't hesitate to scoop her into his arms and move to the enormous bed. Carson could hear his friend talking softly to Fallon as he tucked a cover around her. "Close your eyes for a few minutes, Sweetheart. We'll answer all the questions I can see in them, I promise. Before you drift off, it's important you know how perfect you are for us." Carson couldn't agree more.

By the time he'd taken a quick shower, Silas was waiting in the kitchen with fresh coffee. They stepped out onto the deck facing the river. Before Fallon, Carson had spent little time in the private inner sanctum of the Wests. He'd spent a lot of time designing and programming some of their security systems. Setting up the main suite's shower was one of the perks of specializing in applied computer programming—he'd been able to tweak the original setup to add lights and sound. This was the first time he'd spent any significant amount of personal time ensconced in the Prairie Winds compound.

"This place has to be the nicest damned prison in the world. I can see why Tobi wanted to move outside the secured perimeter." Knowing your every move was being recorded, that every word you spoke outside the confines of your private apartment was being overheard must have been exhausting. Silas nodded his head in agreement.

"We both grew up in very close-knit social environments. Hell, the old saying, everyone knew what you were doing if you couldn't remember was so true of my small enclave, but the joke was lost on half the population. Honestly, I'm more worried about the false sense of security Fallon might get if she lives here too long. Don't get me wrong, I'm thrilled she is safe—but I don't want her to forget there is a real and credible threat lurking too close."

"I hope Lilly can shed some light on what her parents might have been up to. My gut tells me Lilly holds the key that will be our turning point with this mystery. Hagan Brody's background indicates he's a love 'em and leave 'em sort, who wouldn't give a rat's ass if a woman walked out, so what's his end-game?"

"From what Tobi said, he seemed to be answering to someone else. It will be important to find out who is pulling the strings." Silas finished Carson's thoughts with his usual precision. The two of them had been friends long enough to understand how the other one would react and interpret information in most situations.

"Let's get some sleep. I noticed Fallon was restless when I checked on her before coming out here. I can't tell you how pleased I am that she sleeps so well between us. She may seem unfazed by everything that's happened to her, but I think she has been so focused on getting through school, dealing with the grief of losing her parents, and building a career, she is ignoring the pain. She'll continue to push anything remotely resembling distress or fear to the back of her mind until something snaps." Silas agreed but was surprised Carson had made such an in-depth observation. Carson usually saw things in black and white with very little falling into the gray area most people labeled as feelings. Smiling to himself, Silas counted it as another sign Fallon was the one they'd been waiting for.

Chapter Fifteen

L ILLY WEST LEANED back against the rattan chair, lifting a highball glass to her lips, but Fallon knew the amber liquid was iced tea. When she'd teased the other woman, Lilly had laughed. "Those boys of mine complained to the dads because my friends and I had a margarita party a couple of months ago down in Austin. Okay, it got a little out of hand, and a couple of us fell off one of the bridges down on the river walk. Holy hell, that water was cold." Waving her hands as if they would erase the memory, she giggled before continuing.

"I don't know how they got their damned hands on that blasted security tape, but they did. I'm telling you former Special Forces operators must get some sort of infusion of super sleuth they never outgrow. Their network of friends is so huge it's positively alarming, and a bigger group of tattletales you'll never encounter, I promise you. Anyway, after they whined to my husbands, I've seized every opportunity to feed their hysteria just to make them look ludicrous. It's so much fun to make them look ridiculous when Del and Dean can tell I'm perfectly sober when they come to rescue me. This is the third time this week I've had a chance to mess with my sons' over-the-top meddling. When the others show up later, I might go for four and set a new record."

Fallon burst out laughing. It was easy to see why Lilly

and her mother had been friends. They were both completely aware of their power over the men in their lives and had no qualms about using it. At the same time, everything about Lilly West screamed honesty. On the few occasions Fallon met her, Lilly always radiated beauty from the inside out. More importantly, the other woman had always been as genuine as anyone Fallon had ever met.

Sensing Fallon's need to move their conversation along, Lilly reached over to pat Fallon's hand. "I know you want answers, Fallon. And you deserve them. I hope I can help." Taking a deep breath, Lilly didn't seem to choose her words as much as she was letting go of any lingering feeling she was betraying a long-held confidence. "Your mom knew I only agreed to protect their secrets as long as you were safe. I made it clear before she ever confided in me, nothing was sacred if you were in danger." Fallon was sure she hadn't done a good job of hiding her surprise because her mother's friend grinned.

"I have paperwork for you, Fallon. Insurance policies I'm sure you don't know about, assets that wouldn't have shown up in any of the court's searches. I know you've started to suspect your parents' jobs were cover stories, and you're right. They worked for multiple agencies in various countries. Keep in mind those groups often have competing agendas. They eventually landed too high on a hit list to escape the consequences."

"How? Why?" Fallon felt like someone had pulled the rug out from under her... again. "Was anything they said the truth?"

"Their love for you was as real as any I've ever seen. They tried to get out of the business a few times when you were young, but they were too valuable to let go. I was listed as your mother's sister on all their paperwork, so you'd have come to me immediately if anything happened to them. When it became clear, the danger was ramping up as a result of their attempts to retire, they reluctantly agreed to stay, but I knew they'd lost faith in what they'd always seen as their mission."

Fallon's head was spinning. When she realized there were black dots dancing in her vision, she took a deep breath, hoping to bring herself back to an even keel. Pulling in another deep breath, Fallon felt Lilly's hand brush away a strand of hair that had blown over her face.

"I'm sorry. I tend to blurt out information when I know it's going to be unpleasant. I supposed it comes from spending so much time surrounded by alpha men. They all seem to believe ripping off the bandage in one fell swoop is better than nudging it gently away from tender tissues. Just so we're clear, I'm absolutely throwing them under this bus." Fallon felt her heart melt. Lilly West was a mother to the depths of her soul—she was doing everything she could to make things easier for Fallon, though the task seemed impossible.

"Do you have any idea what they were working on before their accident?" An accident Fallon had questioned. Local authorities had been quick to assure her they'd thoroughly investigated the incident and found no evidence of foul play.

"I'm not sure it's relevant, but your mom mentioned they were working domestically for the first time in several years. When I asked her how it was going, she didn't seem enthused about working closer to home as I'd expected. She made a vague reference to price-fixing among pharmaceutical companies, but I got the impression that wasn't the only issue." Lilly paused, lost in thought for several seconds before the cloud of a sad memory passed.

"I want you to know how much I appreciate you extending your friendship with my mother to include me." Fallon felt her cheeks heat with embarrassment. She hadn't intended to make the confession, it just slipped out before she could hold the words back.

"Oh honey, it's my great honor and privilege. You were the apple of your parents' eyes despite their poor career choice. They adored you, and it's easy to see why. Your mom and dad were so proud of your success." Leaning close, Lilly asked, "Do you have any idea what your dad might have put inside the puzzle?"

"No. To be honest, I hadn't thought about it until my conversation with Tobi. I brought it with me... I brought everything that I considered important. The car I bought wasn't huge, but it was large enough to hold what little I had. It wasn't like I'd had time to collect much. My apartment was rented furnished, most of my college textbooks were digital, and I kept very little of the personal possessions I found in my parents' house." She grinned, "Our tastes never seemed to align. They bought unusual items from around the world, but most of those mementos were what I would call trinkets. Knowing what I know now, I wonder if all those cute but useless things were bought more to look like tourists than anything else." Lilly didn't respond right away, giving Fallon time to sort through her thoughts.

Sorting out her parents' meager belongings after their death was a hazy memory Fallon pushed to the back of her mind as quickly as possible. Now she knew she'd been incredibly naïve. Her mom and dad had both worked as long as she could remember. Maybe it should have seemed odd they didn't have more material possessions, but it hadn't. Some of the things she remembered as a child had been missing, but she'd assumed her clutter-phobic mother had gone on one of her purging binges. After everything she was learning about their secret life, Fallon realized she was questioning everything.

"Don't question their love, Fallon." She was startled to realize the other woman had practically read her mind. "Don't look so surprised, dear. It was written all over your face. My sons are secretive as hell with the contract missions their team takes on. I didn't know they were doing contract work for a long time." Lilly looked off into the distance, and Fallon knew they'd made a connection she hadn't expected. The older woman had obviously felt left out of her son's inner circle of confidence. Lilly was no stranger to the uncomfortable feelings Fallon was experiencing. It was a strange mixture of loneliness while surrounded by others and betrayal.

Shaking her head, Lilly flashed a smile and shrugged, "I decided that making lemonade was a waste of my skill set. Now a lemon launcher? Much more fun. As part of their penance, I made sure Kent and Kyle included me in their weapons training classes. I danced for joy when they hired a demolitions specialist. I can't tell you how therapeutic it is to blow something up." For the next half hour, Lilly regaled Fallon with stories about explosions and weapons.

It hadn't taken long for Fallon to understand the younger Wests' concerns about their mother's wild west mentality. It was hard to imagine the elegant and always posh-dressed woman who'd been her mother's friend as a crack shot. In the end, Fallon had been mopping her eyes, the tears from her laughter doing wonders for her spirit. She'd spent so much time during the past couple of years worrying about trying to stumble her way blindly through life as she struggled to work her way through the mind-numbing grief, Fallon had somehow forgotten how important it was to live—really live in the moment.

Laughter rang out over the grassy area between what Tobi called the Forum Shops and the spacious gazebo. The sound of their giggling friends drew Fallon and Lilly's attention. Before they were inundated with chattering women, Fallon took Lilly's hand in her own. "I'm grateful for your help, Lilly. I know this conversation wasn't easy for you, and I appreciate how open you've been with me." As they stood to greet the approaching group, Lilly hugged her close and discreetly slipped an envelope into her hand.

"The boys agreed to turn off the sound equipment while we were alone, but they insisted they be able to see us at all times. I didn't want you to feel you had to share everything with them until you were ready." Fallon noted Lilly shifted her position, so her back was to a camera Fallon noticed earlier. "Never underestimate the skills of the Prairie Winds Team, Fallon. They are the best at what they do, and that includes lip-reading. This is the information I mentioned earlier." Wrapping her arms around Fallon in a fierce hug, Lilly whispered, "Give Carson and Silas a chance. They're wonderful men and have been waiting a long time for a woman to love."

Before Fallon could respond, they were swarmed by more laughter and greetings than Fallon could track. Names were thrown out along with their connection to Tobi, Lilly, or the club. She noted two women quietly admitted they were new members of the teams. Ordinarily, Fallon was good with names, but the buzz of energy along with the rapid-fire information was overwhelming.

"Oh, hell, I'm never going to remember every one of your names. Please don't be offended when I ask you again later. I swear I'm not usually this disconnected." Juggling multiple tasks and projects simultaneously was something she'd always taken pride in, but today it felt like her life was spinning faster than her mind could process.

"No one will mind, I promise. We're a lot on anyone's best day, and from what I've heard, you have a lot going on. Enjoy the margaritas while you can because the next batch will make your liver want to run and hide. Tobi's mixes on the curve." Fallon recognized the pretty Latina as Tobi's friend and business partner, Gracie.

"Curve? There's a curve for mixing margaritas?" Fallon snickered at the unusual reference to teaching.

"It's a damned steep curve, too. She knows the men won't leave us alone for long, so it's important to ramp things up quickly. Heaven forbid anyone would walk out on their own. I swear she enjoys winding up the Doms."

"What the hell is that?" A woman Fallon remembered introducing herself as Jen pointed at a speck on the horizon. Fallon didn't know what it was, but it was damned impressed Jen had spotted it while it was so far away. Squinting, Fallon noted whatever the other woman saw, the damned thing was moving rapidly in their direction.

"Oh shit. The guys are going to be pissed. There's a no-fly zone over this entire area high enough you'll run into the pearly gates before you can glide over the compound." Fallon watched several of the women reach for various pieces of jewelry they wore. She focused on Jen's fingers, watching her depress a recessed button hidden in one of the chain links of the diamond-studded piece. The other woman must have noticed her interest. Grinning, she gave Fallon a saucy wink. "Sometimes our men seem over the top in their attempts to keep us safe, and then things like this happen, and I'm grateful for their care."

Fallon raised a brow in question, but it was Tobi who

answered the unspoken inquiry. "All of us pressing our alarms at the same time... oh hell to the yeah. Watch and see, it's going to bring every member of the Prairie Winds team flying in here like a legion of avenging angels."

KYLE WEST STARED at the screen in utter disbelief. "Who the fuck launched a drone? Is that thing headed this way? Fucking hell. Drones are Cam's pet project. What time are he and Carl supposed to land? Somebody get Sam McCall on the phone."

"Geez, Kyle, what am I? Chopped liver? I'm devastated you haven't been anxiously awaiting my return, as well. I hope my fragile ego survives." CeCe Barnes stood in the doorway of the main security office, looking every inch the tanned and sex-sated vixen Kyle knew she was.

"CeCe." The warning in Cam's voice lacked conviction as he spoke over his wife's shoulder. Carl Phillips appeared to be working hard to hold back his laughter as he rolled his eyes at the haughty look she gave Kyle. *Dr. Barnes one. Kyle West zero.*

"Your men are teaching you bad habits, Cecelia."

"On that, we agree, although I suspect that's where our collaboration ends." Outside the areas of the club designated for play, the Wests insisted their interactions with members mirror outside social rules of engagement. Before he could respond, alarms lit up the board in front of him, and every man in the room, except the two assigned to the monitors and radios, took off at a dead run. Carl barely wrapped his large hands around CeCe's shoulders, lifting her out of the doorway before the group thundered down the hall.

"What the hell was that about?" As soon as Carl released her, CeCe stepped around him, her attention drawn to the bank of monitors covering one wall. "Damn, this place is amazing. How do two men monitor all these feeds? You guys probably dream in a fourth dimension. If you had medical experience, I swear I'd hire you on the spot." CeCe wasn't easily impressed, but these men were at the top of their game. She was just a casual observer and could see they weren't missing a beat.

"Roger that, boss. Incoming from the south. And, Kyle... heads up, your mom is locked and loaded." The man yanked his headset off and chuckled. Turning to the others in the room, he grinned. "I figured that would rattle his cage a bit. Damn, I love Lilly. She makes my job so much more interesting."

CeCe could only imagine.

Chapter Sixteen

FALLON STOOD AT the rail of the gazebo staring as the black dot on the horizon grew larger. It seemed so small, she didn't understand why everyone perceived it as a threat. Obviously, the other women had a different view. "Don't worry, girls. I got this." Lilly stepped between Fallon and Jen, raising the biggest pistol Fallon had ever seen. Okay, so it was the *only one* she'd ever seen except in the movies, but still.

"Damn, Lilly, I don't think the guys will want you to blow it into a million pieces." Jen's words of warning seemed reasonable to Fallon. What harm could a kiddy plane do, anyway?

"Pieces, hell. She'll vaporize it with that bazooka." Tobi's giggle was followed by the distinct sound of men shouting in the distance.

"Tell those guys to keep their blasted shirts on. I'm not going to shoot it down. I just wanted to scare them a little." Her words were followed by a deafening blast that made Fallon screech in surprise. Lilly glanced her way, her eyes glimmering with mischief. "Sorry, honey, I should have warned you. Bessie here is noisy. She'll put a good-sized hole in you, as well. Of course, I was just playing with that boogie. Kyle would bitch like an old maid at a church social if I roasted the evidence. He gets downright cranky about that sort of thing. I swear he is going to give himself a stroke someday." Seconds later, the man in question was reaching for his mother's weapon.

"Good lord, Mother. Are you trying to give me a stroke? Give me that thing. Do the dads know you have this cannon?" Fallon wasn't sure how Kyle seemed to have materialized from thin air. One second, he'd been running down the sidewalk; the next, he'd hurdled the side of the gazebo, landing directly behind his mother and wife.

"Drop it." Kent West jumped over the railing, landing on both feet in a move that reminded Fallon the men must spend a lot of time training. His tone seemed too harsh, and Fallon was surprised Kent would speak to his mother so rudely. She opened her mouth to speak for Lilly when she noticed the small aircraft landing nearby. A man she didn't recognize stood nearby smiling as he held a small controller.

"Damn, you guys sure know how to welcome a guy home." There was almost surreal confidence surrounding the man with the controller. Fallon wondered who he was and how long he'd been gone. His dark hair and intense eyes made him seem mysterious, but when his gaze landed on her, she didn't sense he was a threat. Until she met Hagan Brody, Fallon considered herself a good judge of character. In some ways, she'd known the two of them would never work out in the long term, but she'd been so lonely after her parents died, she'd ignored the red flags.

"You going to stand over there gloating or shut the damned thing down so the owner doesn't decide he wants it back?" Fallon knew Kyle was speaking to the man she hadn't met, even though his focus was centered on his wife. Kyle gave Tobi a quick kiss that made her giggle like a schoolgirl before casting a scathing look his mother's way, earning an exaggerated eye-roll from Lilly.

"Tobi dear, I don't think your husband is getting enough nooky. He's so cranky, if you could please put out a little extra... well... effort, I'd appreciate it." Lilly pretended to buff her nails on her silk blouse, batting her eyes in such an exaggerated manner it gave the entire scene a cartoon appearance. Kent West pulled the gun from his mother's purse when she discretely tried to hide it. Shaking his head and chuckling to himself, he checked the safety before shoving beneath his belt.

"Notice I'm nice and calm. Tobi likes me best." His muttered words made Tobi giggle as everyone around them burst into riotous laughter.

"Cameron, you certainly know how to make an appearance. I'm not sure what you're holding, but I want to talk to you about it later. It looks like something I could manage, and I'm tired of the college kids having all the fun with drones. Some drones have weapons, right?" Lilly moved closer to the man she'd call Cameron and Fallon wondered if Carl Phillips was nearby as well.

"Jesus, Joseph, and Mary, that's all we need." Kyle turned on his heel and stomped out of the gazebo.

"Ladies, I don't see any reason you can't continue your party, but we'll ask you to move it closer to the house. There's plenty of us to move everything to the pool in one trip." Looking around her, Fallon was surprised to see each of the women standing with at least one man. It wasn't hard to distinguish between those who were simply being watched over by a member of the Wests' team and those who were being protected by their own Doms. For the first time, Fallon understood what Carson and Silas had tried to explain. There was an intense intimacy between the Doms and their submissives—something difficult to define but impossible to miss.

Fallon felt Silas approaching just before his hands wrapped around her upper arms. Turning her slowly, he looked down at her, his gaze filled with concern. "I'm sorry it took us so long to get here. We were at the shooting range. Since you don't have an alarm, we didn't know there was trouble until a few seconds ago." Pulling her close, Silas hugged her tightly against his chest before releasing her to Carson.

"We'll fix the alarm problem in short order, Chef." Carson embraced her, and Fallon didn't miss how much comfort she found in both of their holds. She was over- whelmed by everything happening around her but grateful for the growing connection she felt with both men. "Come on, let's move closer to the house. Kyle and Cam are going to spend hours taking that damned drone apart. You and the others might as well enjoy yourselves."

"And we'll enjoy watching you do it." Silas moved to stand beside Carson, giving his eyebrows a quick wiggle like Snidely Whiplash. "Until we know the drone isn't connected to you, I think it would be best if we didn't let you out of our sight." Fallon wanted to argue but reluctant- ly agreed there was a chance the drone had been looking for her. She'd driven to Austin, then basically vanished. If Hagan was intent on securing the puzzle, he'd need to find her first—though why he didn't simply call seemed odd.

"I wonder whatever happened to my cell phone. To be honest, I forgot all about it. It wasn't much, and I can't say that I've missed it." She shrugged when Tobi and several others looked at her aghast.

"No phone? Are you kidding? I'd lose my mind if I couldn't check on everyone and social media." Tobi paused, tapping a perfectly manicured nail against the side of her lower jaw. "Now that I think about it, maybe it wouldn't be so bad. God knows I'd have a lot more free time and money since I wouldn't be shopping online when I was bored. I'll bet those plain phones are harder to track, as well." It took them less than a minute to move from the gazebo to the pool area, and they'd continued their discussion about the merits of phones as they moved along.

"Definitely a perk." Jen dropped into a chaise lounge and leaned back, her long legs extended with her ankles crossed. "I get the whole safety issue, I really do. I was kidnapped, and it sucked. As the kids say, *do not recommend.*" Fallon remained silent as Jen seemed lost in thought before shaking off the momentary disconnection. "Now, our panic alarms are more powerful and more likely to be overlooked by anyone with nefarious intentions." Fallon felt her eyes widen despite her best effort to remain impassive. She heard Carson's low chuckle as he and Silas kissed her cheeks and moved to the side.

"Jen's a smart girl. I mean, like a really, really smart girl. Nerdy smart." Gracie's response made Jen blush. "Everybody expects CeCe to be super smart because she is a surgeon, but tall, blonde and gorgeous over here takes people by surprise. They never see her coming. I've never seen her start something she didn't master. Smack, I might be jealous if I didn't like her so much." Lifting her margarita, Gracie leaned forward to clink her glass against Jen's in a toast to the power of friendship.

"Smack? I swear you really should stop eavesdropping on your kids. You pick up their slang, but not the correct context." Gracie frowned before shrugging off Tobi's comment.

"All kidding aside, Fallon. You're going to love it here. I did not know how incredible real friendship could be before coming to Prairie Winds. The members of the club are screened within an inch of their lives, so it's unusual to meet someone who is anything other than what you see." Fallon smiled at Gracie's odd way of phrasing things. The woman's Spanish accent was faint but enough to let Fallon know English wasn't her first language.

"That's not to say bitches don't walk among us because that sort of behavior is damned hard to detect in the sort of testing and rigorous background checks members go through. In general, the subs sort through them fairly quickly." Fallon didn't know Jen well but didn't miss her sarcasm.

"Kent and Kyle don't have the time or inclination to deal with petty nonsense, so any member exhibiting questionable behavior has their membership revoked quickly." Tobi's gaze moved to a young woman standing to the side of the pool deck. Fallon followed the other woman's gaze, surprised to see her staring intently at Carson. When Fallon looked back at Tobi, the pretty blonde frowned. "I'm not sure how she ended up at this party. I didn't call her."

"She was standing outside the office yesterday when we were talking about getting together. Micah told me she mentioned how anxious she was to make friends at the club, and he agreed this would be an opportunity for her to meet people. I told him that was a mistake. She is only here for one reason... Carson. I'm telling you the woman is obsessed." Gracie pulled her chair around, so her back was to the man standing watch over the group. "Nancy Dressler comes from the same small town where Carson grew up. She moved here because she knows he has money. I heard her telling one of the other subs how she was willing to put up with Silas as long as she had access to their bank accounts."

"I don't want to get involved in any love triangles… or whatever shape it might be with four people."

"That would be a square, dear." Lilly moved closer, giving Fallon a mischievous grin. "I'm sorry, that was too easy, and I'm cranky because Kent took my gun. Now I wish I'd blown that damned drone into a million pieces. This is what I get for behaving. There's no future in it, I tell you. As for Nancy, she is a couple of sandwiches short of a picnic. She keeps trying to get Carson's attention, but he wants nothing to do with her. I'll let him tell you the story, but I don't want you to worry about him being taken, no matter what she might try to tell you." Patting Fallon's hand, she added, "I'd have never picked them for you unless I knew they were available."

Fallon let out a sigh of relief. She'd forgotten Lilly was responsible for Carson and Silas being on their way to the club the afternoon they met. Arranging for them to be her escorts that night should have been all the endorsement Fallon needed. She felt her face flush with shame, knowing it looked as though she hadn't trusted Lilly's judgment. Her whispered apology was met with a shake of Lilly's head.

"Don't worry. I'd have been surprised if you *did* remember. After all, you've had a harrowing few days on top of a disastrous couple of months. Your heart will be safe in Silas and Carson's care. I'm not saying you'll end up with them… that's up to the three of you to work out. I'm only saying they are honest men who are so taken with you anyone can see they are off the market."

"But does Nancy know? It doesn't look like she got the memo." Gracie's whispered question was followed quickly by Jen's giggling addition.

"The bigger question is...will she care?" Jen's eyes moved to the pool area's entrance sparkling with amusement, making Fallon wonder who'd shown up. Spending time with the Prairie Winds women was turning out to be a lot like being strapped to a tilt-a-whirl on steroids. Fallon felt the rise and fall of the ride while being spun in circles as she tried to track conversations and keep up with the growing list of details about other members. Having always lived in large cities, Fallon often wondered about small-town living. She read about communities where everyone knew one another, but the concept was so foreign to her it seemed impossible. Austin wasn't a small town, but the club appeared to be a community all on its own. *Damn, I'm going to have to take notes at this rate.*

"Are you Fallon?" Before she could respond, the gorgeous woman with dancing dark eyes, who seemed to have materialized from thin air, extended her hand. "I'm CeCe Barnes, and Brooks tells me you're a pharmacist. I wanted to introduce myself. I've been trying to find the right person to operate the pharmacy I'm building in the area between the clinic and surgical center. He tells me you might be interested. If that's right, I'd like to set up a meet and greet. We don't have to do it today... tomorrow morning is fine."

"Take a breath, Pet." A man Fallon suspected everyone viewed as tall, dark, and dangerous stepped up behind the whirlwind who'd introduced herself as CeCe. Smiling at Fallon, the man pulled CeCe back against his chest. "We only landed an hour ago, and you're already networking. I'd be impressed if I hadn't seen the shell-shocked look on Fallon's face." The man extended his hand, grasping hers in a hold that was surprisingly gentle. "It's nice to finally meet you, Fallon. I'm Cameron Barnes. I was a friend of your father's before he and your mother married. While we were in the same line of work, we didn't work together." Fallon wasn't sure exactly how to interpret his remark. There was an air of authority surrounding the man that made her hesitant to ask questions. She'd seen him earlier with the drone controller and wondered what happened to the toy that seemed to cause such a stir.

When a second man moved to CeCe's other side, Fallon wondered if the blue-eyed blonde was the famous surgeon's second Dom. His warm smile immediately put Fallon at ease. "Hi, Fallon, I'm Carl Phillips. I hope our little steamroller didn't scare you off. She was excited to hear you might be interested in joining her team."

"I've run into a snag transferring my license—I hope to get the issue resolved soon."

"I think you'll find the issue is resolved very soon. Prairie Winds members help one another, and we've got a fair amount of influence." Carl Phillips's blue eyes shone with knowledge, and she felt as though she'd been given a quick glimpse into how tight the Prairie Winds group was and how much they looked out for one another. "I know there are a lot of people clamoring for your time," Carl gave CeCe a panty-melting smile before returning his attention to Fallon, "but I'm going to push my way to the front of the line. I'd like to speak with you later this evening about the puzzle your father gave you. Getting some background information about your relationship will help me solve it. The code is usually something personal... a favorite childhood story, grandmother's name, nickname, or something similar. The more insight I have into your relationship, the faster I can work out the solution."

Fallon nodded her understanding. It was humbling to admit how little time she's spent trying to figure out to open the puzzle. Her world had imploded so quickly after her dad gave it to her there was an underlying negative connection for her. Fallon hadn't bothered taking the gift out of her suitcase—she'd stuffed the battered bag in the top of her closet and forgotten about it until she'd moved to Texas. If Hagen hadn't been able to find the puzzle, it was probably because the bag looked worse for wear. Hagen Brody was a snob of the first order. He'd have overlooked the bag, not giving it any consideration because of its condition and lack of a designer label.

"What Carl is tactfully trying to convey without saying it outright is, don't get wasted this afternoon. While a few drinks might be helpful, relaxing you enough to let slip pieces of information he'd find useful, too much a good thing would be counterproductive. Depending on your tolerance, I'd advise you to err on the side of the angels. Tobi's margaritas will kick your ass from here to next Tuesday if you don't watch yourself. The second one will make you spill all your secrets. After that, your thoughts will be too chaotic to prioritize." CeCe was grinning from ear to ear as Cameron Barnes stood beside her shaking his head.

"Pet, I swear to everything holy your filter is teetering between flawed and nonexistent." Cameron might think he was fooling Fallon with his stern demeanor, but she heard the underlying amusement in his voice.

"Geez, Cam, you're pretty cranky for a man who just returned from vacation." Tobi set a tray of margaritas on a nearby table and laughed.

"When I find out who gave Lilly the code to my sat-phone, there's going to be hell to pay. She's been calling me ever since Fallon hit town." Fallon wasn't sure why she was surprised. Lilly West was a mother to the depth of her soul. She would protect anyone she believed was one of hers. Tobi laughed out loud as several other women winced.

"If Lilly has your number, she got it from my son. Damn, that kid is amazing. I got a look at his contact list one day—it reads like a Spies-R-Us Who's Who in the Zoo list." Taking a gulp of the frozen concoction in front of her. Everyone around her laughed when her eyes widened in surprise as a shudder appeared to start in her core before quaking its way to the surface. Fallon understood... she'd only taken a sip of hers and swore her vision dimmed for a few seconds. As a bartender, she respected the woman's ability to blend the killer mix her friends were drinking at an alarming rate. Tobi seemed to shake off the effects, refocusing on Cameron Barnes.

"It won't do you any good to change it. He'll have it again before sunset. If it was his sister, I'd say it might be a problem. She'd be selling the contacts on e-Bay." Fallon knew the Wests had twins, but she hadn't met them yet. Recognizing Lilly's and Tobi's strength made Fallon curious about what the next generation was bringing to the table.

Chapter Seventeen

C ARSON LEANED BACK against the warm brick of the club's back wall, listening to Tobi talk about her son's computer skills, and shook his head. For the first time, he had a very real understanding of what his own mother must have faced before she'd died. Tobi was struggling to find a balance between being proud of her son's skills and her concern about how the kid's talent could be used. He made a mental note to speak with Kameron West's parents about a mentoring program his company was starting. The young man didn't need their technical help, but guiding him through the choppy waters where ethics and money pulled techs in opposite directions might well make all the difference.

"He'd be a good candidate for your mentoring program." Carson wasn't surprised Silas had come to the same conclusion. They were often on the same page, so he wasn't surprised to hear his friend had picked up on the conversation's undercurrent. "Watching Fallon make a million mental notes, cataloging little pieces of information about her new friends gives me a lot of hope she'll stick around. If she was planning to move on, it wouldn't be worth the effort."

"I agree. It's encouraging." Knowing CeCe wanted to talk to Fallon about the in-house pharmacy she was building was also a huge plus since she wouldn't be pounding the pavement looking for a job. Working in a private clinic surrounded by like-minded people was the best possible solution since their home was less than a mile from the facility. Kyle West stepped into the pool area from a nearby door and motioned them inside.

"We've talked to the kid who owns the drone. He's local and far too trusting. He was about a mile down the road practicing with his new drone when a man approached him. The guy offered to help him learn to fly the bird. The kid is one of our son's friends, so he's aware of the no-fly zone over the compound. Kevin told the man he couldn't fly over our property, but he refused to turn back. He'd already texted Kam to let him know what was happening because Kevin saw Grandma Lilly on the drone's monitor and didn't want her to blow up his birthday present." Kent had joined them and stood nearby chuckling.

"Kevin might have been fooled by the stranger who offered to help, but he recognized the real threat." Kent's assessment was probably more accurate than any of them knew.

"We've shown Kevin a picture of Hagan Brody. He confirmed Brody is the man who flew the drone." Kyle paused, frowning before he added, "Brody linked his phone to the damned thing and downloaded the footage before we could stop him." Carson could see the lines of frustration forming at the corners of Kyle's eyes. The man didn't like being outdone by an adversary, and that was exactly how he was viewing this incident.

"Do we know where he's staying? It seems likely he's checked into a nearby hotel. Nothing in his file would lead me to believe he has any experience camping." Carson tried to hold back his smile. Hagen Brody's file showed he was a top-shelf pansy-ass who probably got a rash if he had to walk more than a block outside to get into his sports car.

"We checked registrations but didn't come up with anything under his name. Team members are canvasing the most likely spots. We'll flash his picture around and see what turns up. I'd like to enlist local law enforcement. Unfortunately, he has done nothing illegal. He'll plead ignorance about the no-fly zone, and following an ex across the country isn't a crime. He'll claim he's here to beg forgiveness and win her back. Until he does something overtly illegal, law enforcements' hands are tied." Kyle's frustration was clear.

"We, however, operate by a different set of rules." Kent's eyes gleamed with intent. "Cam thinks her dad hid evidence in the puzzle... something he would have considered insurance."

"It would explain Brody's persistence because, despite her amazing appeal, I don't believe the man cares about anyone but himself." Silas had moved so he could continue watching Fallon through one of the floor-to-ceiling windows. After the drone incident, Carson understood his friend's reluctance to let her out of their sight. "She agreed to spend some time with Carl later. Hopefully, they'll be able to work together on the puzzle's solution. From what I've learned, anything inside the cylinder could be destroyed if the solution isn't entered correctly after a set number of tries."

"In this instance, Hollywood was off the mark. Cryptex puzzles like the one Fallon's dad would have used have a different purpose. He wanted her to have whatever is inside, so it's unlikely he would set it up to destroy the message if the wrong answer is entered the first time." The group of men gathered around was growing as members of the team moved closer. Carson was pleased when the new members of the special operations teams stepped forward to offer their help outside their assigned duties. Knowing Fallon would have additional support if needed would go a long way to make certain she was safe.

Watching Fallon sip the drink Tobi set in front of her, Carson shook his head in amusement. She'd worked at a bar to pay her way through college, so she was no stranger to the scene, but she obviously wasn't much of a drinker herself. They'd let her enjoy the party for a little longer before she answered Carl's questions.

The plan was for the conversation to take place in one of the larger seating areas in the club's main room. Limiting the number of people surrounding Fallon was a double-edged sword. Ensuring she was comfortable enough to speak freely was paramount. At the other end of the spectrum, they knew the more people who could hear what she had to say, the more likely it was someone in the group would figure out the puzzle's solution. Since it was a numbers game, they arranged things so anyone else who might contribute would gather in the control room to brainstorm.

Micah Drake stepped into the circle, his expression dark as he handed a sheet of paper to Kyle before distributing the rest to Carson, Silas, Jax, and Sam McCall. "When we knew Fallon was on her way to Texas, I set up a few alerts on the dark web, as well as the one the general public uses. Before you ask... no, this isn't something we always do, but it isn't particularly unusual either. Since we didn't have the same level of background information we have when we recruit, I made certain we used all the alerts at my disposal."

Carson couldn't argue with Micah's logic. The man

had been with the Wests since they first started the club and special teams—he was their head of security for a good reason. Micah was also a gifted empath who understood the value of trusting his instincts. Skimming over the information he had been handed, Carson was grateful Micah had made an effort to ferret out anything he could find.

"It appears the rumors are true." Cam Barnes stared at the paper in his hands, the firm line of his mouth the only indication he was anything other than his usual calm, collected self. Sighing loud enough to draw questioning looks from the men surrounding him, Cam reluctantly added, "I'd heard the Fosters were close to shutting down an enormous drug import business. Everyone always assumed that was why they were taken out."

"Fallon believes her parents were killed in a car accident." Even as Carson spoke the words, he realized how naïve they sounded.

"I'm sure she does, although I'd guess she is less convinced now. No one from the agency would have told her the truth for too many reasons to list—chief among them her safety. Until now, being unaware was in her best interest."

"How did anyone know she had the puzzle?" Silas asked without taking his eyes off the group of women laughing beside the pool.

"I have no idea, but the most likely scenario is her dad was being watched. Her father wasn't known for being cautious, and his impending retirement probably had made him lackadaisical. If he hadn't already been planning to leave the agency, the decision would have been made for him. His heart just wasn't in it any longer—a feeling I understand all too well. An agent is only as good as his performance on his worst day. Halfway in is never an option." Carson felt as though Cam was talking as much about himself as he was Fallon's father.

"Cryptic, but not hard to sort out. I swear the dark web is being taken over by junior high school kids." Carson understood Cam's frustration. What started out as a sinister side of the internet was morphing into a place for extremists and kids. "Hagen Brody is nothing more than a means to an end. He's already a marked man, whether or not he retrieves whatever is in that puzzle. My best guess? There is a list of contacts or suppliers inside the puzzle. I only hope there's evidence to back up whatever we find because a simple list of names won't be enough to protect Fallon."

"If you can't get them off the streets, they may still target her—either for revenge or out of concern she has more information hidden away." Silas frowned as he took another look at the paper in his hand. "Let's get her in here and see if we can figure out the solution to the puzzle."

FALLON LEANED BACK against the back of the leather sofa and sighed. "I got hit by a truck and didn't feel this spent." She gave Carson and Silas a wry smile hoping they understood she was teasing rather than complaining. Fallon had never made many friends outside work. The few people she'd gotten to know at the bar had been ruthless in their teasing. Her coworkers at the pharmacy had been so intimidated by the store's management, they'd been afraid to speak to one another.

During the long drive to Texas, Fallon promised herself she'd find a better work environment this time around.

The short time she'd spent with Dr. Cecelia Barnes was encouraging, but Fallon held back her enthusiasm. After the fiasco of her last job, she'd learned how quickly her career could be derailed when she made a hasty decision. She'd cursed herself a thousand times for not recognizing the job offer from Brody Pharmaceuticals was too good to be true.

"She's done." Something about the tone of Silas's voice pulled Fallon back to the moment.

"Yeah, I can see she has checked out." Blinking to bring Carl Phillips into focus, Fallon tried to straighten her spine and wondered when Carson had pulled her onto his lap.

"Stay where I put you, Chef." Carson's arms tightened enough to reinforce his warning.

"I'm sorry. It seems Tobi's margarita reputation is well earned." Her lame attempt to make light of the situation earned her a sympathetic smile from Carl, but she could see he would not relent.

"I have plenty of information to start. Let me review everything and brainstorm with a friend in Montana. If Tobi hasn't pickled Jen's brain, I will bring her in as well. She thinks laterally and views the world differently than most people. I know it drives Sam and Sage crazy at times, but she's often remarkably helpful sorting through puzzles."

"Well, good luck with that. When I came in a few minutes ago, she was dancing naked on the diving board. When Sam tried to pull her back onto the pool deck, they both ended up in the water." Fallon looked up to see a man grinning at her despite his remarks being directed to Carl." Everyone around them laughed, leaving Fallon curious about the inside joke. Her expression must have given away her confusion because the man gave her a quick wink. "My brother isn't as much fun as I am, Fallon. I'm Sage McCall. It takes both of us to keep up with Jen."

It was easy to see the man was crazy about the wild child he'd married. It hadn't taken Fallon long to see Jen was a free spirit who marched to a beat only she could hear. The women she'd met all seemed to share the same independent mindset. They might be sexually submissive, but that appeared to be where they drew the line. In the short time she'd been in Texas, Fallon was quickly falling in love with the state. The wide-open spaces, clean air, and friendly people were just a few of the things she loved about the Lone Star State.

Fallon was so lost in her own thoughts she didn't notice Silas and Carson leading her to the elevator. The doors sliding closed caught her attention a heartbeat before a stinging swat lit her ass on fire.

"Fucking hell. What was that for?" She'd barely spit the words out before another swat rocked her up onto her toes. "Damn it, stop that. What's wrong with you two? Why don't you just tell me what I did that seems to have incensed you to the point of physical violence."

"Don't confuse a couple of swats with physical violence. You know enough about the lifestyle to recognize the difference. Your accusation is unfounded. Remember our conversation about situational awareness? Being aware of your surroundings is important, Fallon. You did not know we'd led you into the elevator, did you?" Without waiting for her to respond, he continued snarling, "This is exactly the type of safety issue we've been talking to you about." Carson's voice was tight with frustration, and if she was honest with herself, Fallon knew the first swat was to get her attention, and the second had been a warning about her language. It was ironic because she rarely cursed, but something about the situation rattled her enough to make her behave inappropriately.

"You're too smart to talk like a drunken sailor, Chef. It's beneath you." Carson's comments were more effective than a swat ever could be. Her parents had often said the same thing to her. They'd encouraged her to speak professionally from the time she'd started junior high school. When her friends were using language as a way to rebel, she'd been reminded cursing was a sign of laziness. Using slang words others coined didn't show mastery of expression because it was little more than mimicking others.

"I'm sorry. You're right." Sighing as they walked through the apartment, Fallon could tell she'd surprised them. She wasn't sure what they'd expected, but an apology was clearly not on the list of responses. "This will probably come as a surprise, but I don't usually curse. It was something my parents discouraged and a habit I've always tried to avoid. The first swat surprised me, and I reacted before stopping to ask what I'd done wrong. In my defense, I'm usually keenly aware of my surroundings. Living in the city makes you hyper-aware. I've let my guard down since arriving in Texas because I feel safe."

Both men turned to face her, their expressions softer than they'd been a few seconds earlier. It didn't surprise her that Silas was the first to speak. He seemed to take the lead when situations required a more delicate approach.

"Sweetheart, that's one of the biggest compliments you could have paid us. Knowing you feel safe with us is exactly as it should be, and we should have spoken to you before reacting to your blind obedience. Knowing you'd simply followed with no awareness of where we were headed is worrisome when we haven't figured out why Hagen Brody is making such an effort to determine your location."

"No one understands why he has made no attempt to contact you. Why hasn't he called your cell phone? The security staff has been monitoring it continually since you arrived, and the only calls have been spammers."

"He doesn't have the number." Silas and Carson stared at her as if she were speaking a foreign language.

"You were dating, and he didn't have your phone number?" Carson clearly found the idea completely unbelievable. "How did he contact you?"

"When I threw the phone he'd given me off a bridge, I didn't keep the number." Smiling to herself, she shrugged. "You have no idea how good it felt to heave that damned phone as far as I could manage. I knew he was tracking the phone when he was right behind me as I left the city. There was no way he could have known I'd changed cars unless he was using the phone." The two of them blinked at her in confusion. She didn't pause long enough for them to ask questions before continuing.

"The car I'd been driving was registered to me, but he'd bought it, so I knew better than to take it when I left. Heck, the thing guzzled gas like a thirsty camel, I'd have run out of money long before arriving in Texas. I sold it at a small dealership where the owner was so happy to get his hands on a high-end sports car, he didn't ask any questions. I had enough money to buy the crappy car you saw on the side of the road, but it didn't leave me enough for motel rooms. I had to decide what was more important, sleeping comfortably or gas money." She tried to chuckle at her own joke but judging from the dark expressions on Silas and Carson's faces, they'd failed to see the humor in her comment. Silas shook his head as he took a deep breath.

Fallon had the distinct impression he was struggling to bring his frustration under control.

"I feel like this is one of the situations my family referred to when they said you should never discount dumb luck."

"Hey. Are you calling me dumb?"

"Sweetheart, there is a difference between being dumb and dumb luck. One is a lack of intelligence—I'd never say such a thing. You're clearly a very bright woman. The other is the luck inexperienced or uninformed people are blessed with when the Universe protects them from their own naivety. Dumb luck lets people stumble blindly through minefields of emotional or physical danger, oblivious to the Universal truth shield surrounding them." Fallon stared at Silas for several seconds, hoping what sounded like English would eventually make sense. When she heard Carson laugh, she turned to him, hoping he would explain what Silas meant.

"Don't look at me, Chef. Silas and I have been friends for years, and I still don't understand what he's saying a lot of the time."

"Oh, for heaven's sake, the two of you act as though I'm speaking some kind of New Age lingo you've never heard before." Silas crossed his arms over his chest in mock frustration as his eyes lit with amusement.

"I can't speak for Carson, but I'm not entirely sure what you said. I'm glad you didn't call me dumb. I'd have taken issue with that. As for the luck part, that seems to have started after I met the two of you, so I'm not sure the Universe is protecting me or testing you." This time it was Silas who was staring, his eyes wide while he tried to determine how much of what she'd said was pure bull shit and how much was a sincere observation.

"Our brilliant woman is perfect. She's going to meet your hippy speak and raise you a heckle or two of scientific mumbo-jumbo." Carson laughed at his own joke, making Fallon giggle as Silas rolled his eyes. Fallon felt some of the earlier tension between them melt away as Carson stepped into the kitchen. Pulling bottles of water from the refrigerator, he opened hers before handing it to her. "Drink up, Chef. You answered a thousand questions tonight and barely touched the water we gave you. Hydration is important. As things heat up, you'll understand why this is something we take seriously."

Fallon had news for him—she already knew. The other women at the party had laughed when she'd commented how early summer started in Texas. They'd explained in terrifying detail how hot it would get once spring turned to summer. When she'd expressed her surprise, they called the sweltering afternoon sun a delightful spring day, her new friends laughed.

"The ladies at the party mentioned something about summers being hot here. I suppose dehydration could be an issue."

"Your friends are right. It's hotter than hell here in the summer, but that wasn't the heat we're talking about. Playing can cause dehydration Chef, and we intend to play before sleeping." Fallon felt her cheeks heat with embarrassment. "Don't." Carson shook his head as he lifted her chin with his fingers. "Don't you dare be embarrassed because you didn't understand what I meant by heating things up. You have so much going on, I'm grateful you haven't said it's too much and folded under the pressure."

"It's been a lot, but I'm stronger than I look, and I don't

give up easily." Fallon paused long enough to pull in a steadying breath before plunging ahead. "Don't discount my determination when I've set my mind to a task... or when I'm going after something I want. You are handling me as though I'm made of spun glass... remember fire tempers steel. I've been dodging life's burning arrows for a long time. I'm... well, I'm tired of holding the shield all alone."

Fallon saw the surprise flash in Silas's eyes a split second before Carson pulled her into a bone-crushing hug. "Don't break her, Carson. Damn." Silas's words were tempered by a note of amusement. "We finally find the perfect woman, and you try to snap her like a twig." Fallon giggled as Carson slowly released his iron grip on her. "Let's go. You have too many clothes on, and my cock is going to explode if I don't get inside you."

Carson leaned forward, putting his shoulder in her mid-section before sprinting to the bedroom. Fallon was laughing so hard by the time he set her on her feet, she could barely stand.

"Clothes off. Now." When she stood to look at Silas, Fallon was surprised to see he was already naked. His cock was fully erect, standing proudly as it bounced against his lower abdomen. The man was tall and well-muscled. His skin was a golden tan with only a hint of a tan line around his waist. "If you keep looking at me like I'm a snack, this play session is going to be over far too soon, Sweetheart. Now strip, or I'm going to show you how little respect I have for the pretty dress you're wearing."

Chapter Eighteen

SILAS WATCHED AS the flash of surprise in Fallon's eyes
was quickly replaced by heat when she realized he had
stripped on the way down the hall. The few seconds it took
her to respond to his command to remove her clothing
gave Carson time to catch up, as well. He found it interesting she left her shoes on until he'd glanced down at the
strappy heels and looked at her in question. Fallon blushed
and shrugged before leaning down to slip the shoes from
her feet.

"You are both so tall… it's so strange, really." Her
voice trailed off, but it was easy to see she wasn't finished.
He had a good idea where she'd been headed but waited
patiently for her to continue. "Having you tower over me
is both intimidating and comforting. I'm not sure how to
explain it."

"One of the great things about D/s relationships is that
you don't have to justify your feelings. All we ask is that
you share them. Communication is the second most
important rule in the lifestyle. The first rule of play is
always… *safe, sane, and consensual.*" Silas was grateful
Fallon had learned enough about D/s relationships to
know the basics. He gave her a reassuring smile when she
nodded in understanding before continuing.

"Reading about the lifestyle and experiencing it
firsthand is so different. I'm trying to reconcile it in my

head, but it's tough to make sense of all the conflicting feelings. My head says I should be independent, but my heart feels safe letting you take charge."

"It isn't as conflicting as it first appears, Chef. It takes a lot of courage to let go, especially when you've been on your own for so long." Carson's eyes never left hers as his fingers trailed along the top of her shoulder before dropping to roll a peaked nipple between his thumb and first finger. Fallon shuddered as the flush of arousal bloomed over her upper chest.

Watching Carson spin her up was damned satisfying. Silas wrapped his arm around Fallon's back, smoothing his palm over the dimples of her lower back before slipping his fingers into the open space at the top of her thighs. Smiling to himself, Silas was thrilled to find the outer lips of her pussy already drenched with her sweet honey.

"So wet and ready. Perfect." Silas pushed the tip of his finger past the wet folds, teasing the sensitive outer edge of her vaginal opening. He loved her soft moan as her knees folded. He and Carson caught her easily. As appealing as it sounded, keeping her sandwiched between while they fucked her standing up wasn't what they'd planned. After all the challenges she'd faced today, Fallon deserved to be pampered. Carson pulled condoms from the bedside table and tossed all but one of them onto the bed.

Moving into position, Carson waggled his eyebrows at Fallon as he rolled the condom on. Beckoning her closer with his fingers, Carson didn't waste time once Fallon was within his reach. Wrapping his hands around her upper arms, Carson lifted Fallon with little effort. Positioning her over his cock, the man grinned like a kid who'd just been given his favorite treat.

"Use your hands to guide me home, Chef. I'm going to settle into your heat and hope like hell I can hold off until Silas is seated in your tight little ass." Silas grabbed the bottle of lube, squirting a generous amount onto his palm. Lubing his fingers and condom-covered cock, Silas didn't waste any time pressing the tips of his fingers against the tight ring of muscles around her rear hole.

"Relax, Sweetheart. Let me in. I promise to make it worth every little burn you feel as your body stretches to accept the pleasure your Doms are giving you." Silas felt the tight ring relax enough that he could push two fingers in almost to the first knuckle. "You're doing great. Take a deep breath and push back against my fingers." He watched as Carson pressed his lips against hers in a kiss so hot the temperature in the room ratcheted up several degrees. Leaning forward, Silas kissed the fleshy part of her ass cheek before nipping it just hard enough to distract her.

"Fucking hell. Whatever you did made her clamp down around me like a damned vice." Silas chuckled at the underlying tone of desperation in Carson's voice. His friend might plan to hold on until they could work together to ensure Fallon's pleasure, but Silas had serious doubts any man could. Fallon was temptation personified. "Stop thinking everything to death and get inside our woman, Silas. Jesus, Joseph, and sweet Mother Mary, she's killing me. Her vaginal walls are rippling around me, pulling me so deep I don't know where she ends, and I begin."

Silas pulled his fingers free, relieved he'd been able to push three fingers into her rear entrance, scissoring them to stretch her enough to be sure his cock wouldn't tear the tender tissues. Using another generous squirt of lube, Silas took his time rubbing the slick gel over his throbbing latex-covered cock. He made a mental note to make their medical reports available to Fallon. Having read her club application, Silas already knew she was on birth control and had recent labs as well. Hell, just thinking about how hot it would be to feel her pussy close around his bare cock was enough to make him wonder how he'd survive it. Pressing his tip against the tight ring of muscles, he leaned forward, so the warm skin of his upper chest pressed against her shoulder blades.

"Let me in, Fallon. Take a deep breath. Release it slowly and push out." He smiled when she nodded. Damn, she was so perfect it was hard to believe they'd finally found her. She sucked in a deep breath and used her body to push out exactly as he'd instructed. He didn't hesitate, pushing in until the rigid ring of his corona moved past her tight outer circle of muscles. Fallon gasped when he pushed through, but it was quickly followed by a sigh as her anal opening closed around him.

"Sweetheart, we need to make sure you're as ready as we are." Silas moved his hand lower, using his fingers to tease her pearly clit out of hiding. Carson helped lift her enough he could roll her taut nipples between his fingers, pulling them hard enough to make Fallon shudder.

"Oh, yeah. Our perfect sub likes this. She went liquid around me. Damn, your heat is next level, Chef." Carson was right. Fallon was everything they'd been looking for and then some. Feeling her body ignite under their hands was ramping up every one of his own responses. Silas could hardly wait to feel her come apart—if they were lucky, maybe she'd scream their names when her orgasm swept her over the edge.

"It's too much. I don't know how the others manage to

keep their sanity. The pleasure is more than I can... Oh my God in heaven." Fallon's response to their alternating rhythm was perfect. As Silas pulled back, Carson surged forward. They'd shared enough women, the movements were second nature, and they matched their movements to the demands they felt from Fallon's body.

Fallon might not realize she was responsible for their pounding pace, but her entire body spoke to them with such unbridled enthusiasm it was easy for them to meet her needs. One of the things Silas disliked about well-trained subs was their belief they should mask their own desire. He didn't want a woman who mirrored his body's needs—he wanted to know their responses were genuine. Fallon's openness, her honest reactions to everything they gave her, was only part of what made her so perfect. He admired her courage and intelligence, as well. She was perfect for them and worth the interminable wait.

He felt the shift in Fallon's energy a fraction of a second before she screamed their names. It was the sweetest sound in the world for a couple of reasons. First, he was reassured they'd given her the release they'd promised. Second, it signaled it was time for them to let go of the tenuous hold he'd had over his own release. Letting his body fall over the edge of pleasure as a searing heat moved from his balls up his spine, setting off fireworks behind his eyes before rocketing back down to send pulses of his release into the empty tip of the condom. The entire process was so fast he barely registered the stages before he slumped forward.

Catching his weight on his elbows before he crushed a collapsed Fallon into Carson, Silas hoped like hell his arms would hold him long enough for his legs to regain enough feeling to stand. Fucking hell, every cell in his body felt like it had been fried from the inside out. He enjoyed training with the Prairie Winds operatives—their programs were brutal. As tough as the physical requirements were, after the first week or two, Silas settled into the regime without batting an eye. He could run five miles with a full pack and still play at the club until the damned placed closed—usually as the sun started peaking over the prairie. Now? He was hunched over Fallon's back, gasping for air like he'd run a marathon on a hot Texas afternoon. He couldn't remember a time when he'd felt more physically drained and emotionally enriched.

When his head stopped spinning, Silas pushed himself off Fallon to stand beside the bed. Looking down, he saw his friend's dazed expression. Judging by Carson's expression, he was as decimated as Silas. The elders in his hippy community in the Rockies warned Silas he'd feel like he'd been run over by a truck when the right woman came into his life, and they'd been right. Staggering to the bathroom on trembling legs, Silas returned with everything needed to clean Fallon's tender pussy lips. She'd sleep much better once he'd wiped away all the evidence of their play and patted the swollen tissues dry.

Smiling to himself when she grumbled in her sleep, he wasn't surprised she'd drifted back into a sound sleep by the time he finished. Tucking her between them, Silas sighed. He couldn't wait to show her the home they'd built, anxiously waiting for her to find her way into their lives. The lakeside retreat was also home to their respective businesses. They'd spent over a year designing the main structure—the process was brutal, but the results were spectacular. If the job with CeCe's medical center worked out, their location would be perfect. Their home was less than a five-minute drive from the sprawling medical complex. Silas was so lost in thought he almost missed the soft flash of an incoming message on his phone.

Silas and Carson silenced their phones and muted messages before returning upstairs with Fallon, but their efforts were no match for Micah Drake's wizardry. Carson often commented how he'd love to hire the man away from the Wests but knew mentioning it would be tantamount to treason. Silas silently cursed when he read the message from Kent. He'd hoped Carl Phillips would be able to solve the puzzle—but hadn't expected the man to open the damned cryptex so quickly. By the time Silas sat up, Carson was already looking at his own phone.

As much as he dreaded waking Fallon when she was resting so comfortably, but there wasn't a chance in hell he would cut her out of this meeting. He and Carson had both had their hands on her seconds earlier, and she'd cuddled closer, but the moment he spoke her name, Fallon's eyes opened, and she was scrambling from the bed. *What the hell?* He didn't think she was fully awake as she searched frantically for her clothes.

"Sweetheart, slow down. The place isn't on fire." His calming tone did very little to settle her frantic movements.

"Fallon, stop." Carson's command was stern, but he hadn't raised his voice. It was satisfying to watch her freeze in place, leaving little doubt Fallon Foster was a natural submissive. Her nature was perfect for them but also allowed people to manipulate her if her well-being wasn't their first concern. Frowning to himself, Silas made a mental note to talk to Carson about how they could protect her without stifling her independence. "Kent asked us to come downstairs because Carl solved the puzzle. He didn't pull the parchment from the cylinder because he felt it was something you should do. Fallon blinked several times, trying to bring the world around her into focus before things must have started falling into place.

"He solved the puzzle? Already? Wow." Fallon shook her head as if the sharp movement would dislodge the cobwebs from her mind. "How long was I asleep?" Glancing at a nearby alarm clock, Fallon frowned. "Wait. We've only been upstairs for a... well, not that long considering most of the time was spent playing mattress mambo. Obvious his reputation as a master at this sort of thing is well earned." She'd resumed her frantic search for clothing, tossing their discarded pieces onto the bed as she looked for something to wear. "Oh, for heaven's sake, what am I doing? I can't wear the same thing downstairs. Holy hell, I wonder if mind-blowing orgasms always render people dim-witted? If I spend very much time with the two of you, I'll be sitting in the corner babbling incoherently and eating pudding with my fingers."

Silas gave up trying to keep a straight face and burst out laughing. Carson was grinning like the cat who'd swallowed the canary as he pulled a clean pair of jeans from the dresser. "Chef, your clothes are in the closet." Silas regained his composure, dressing quickly, then leaning against the door frame, watching Fallon search each of the drawers in the enormous walk-in closet.

"What are you looking for, Sweetheart?"

"Underwear. All of my panties and bras are gone. What the heck is that about?" Looking at the jeans and shirt in her hand, she tilted her head to the side, and he could practically hear the questions racing through her mind. "Whose are these? Holy Helen of Troy. I almost put on someone else's clothes. Yikes."

"Those are yours, Chef, Lilly suggested a personal

shopper, and she's been hard at work making certain you have everything you'll need." Carson's comment earned him a look that was too close to a glare for the man to ignore. "Be careful with that look, Fallon. Glaring at one of your Doms is never a good idea. Hell, glaring at any Dom is going to mean trouble."

"Usually in the form of a paddling." Silas straightened from the door's edge and walked into the closet. "We don't consider panties and bras necessary when you are in the club or in your own home. The ones we wanted for you need to be special ordered. They'll be here tomorrow. We won't tolerate any argument about the clothing situation, so don't even start. It's our pleasure and privilege to buy you pretty things."

"We've waited for our own woman for a long time. We are going to enjoy spoiling you—whether it's with clothes, jewelry, or attention. Don't deny us the opportunity." Silas was pleased with Carson's softer approach. The man wasn't always known for diplomacy, but he'd read Fallon perfectly.

"Pick out something to wear, and let's get downstairs before Kyle brings the whole group upstairs. I'd much rather meet them in their office so we can leave when we want to." Fallon giggled as she pulled the jeans up her slender legs.

"I get it. If they're up here, we have to wait for them to decide the discussion is over—sort of like when your friends come over for dinner and a movie, then hang out for hours talking to your parents. You can't go to bed because it's rude, but your so bored you can hear your hair growing." Silas grinned because she'd actually nailed it. Fallon understood precisely what he'd meant while Carson stood by, looking completely confused.

"I swear the world would be a better place if people were all raised in the swamp in a huge Cajun family with no respect for personal boundaries. I don't have any qualms whatsoever about going to bed and leaving people chatting in the living room." When Silas and Fallon didn't respond, Carson shrugged. "Your way seems easier, but it's important you understand having a bunch of sexual Dominants outside your bedroom door will not stop me from settling between your smooth thighs the minute I get naked and horizontal on the bed again." Carson turned on his heel and walked out of the closet. Silas had to stifle his laughter when he looked at Fallon to see her mouth gaping open in shock.

One thing for sure, life with the two of them would never be dull.

Chapter Nineteen

F ALLON STARED AT the letter in her hand, hoping the words would stop swirling around on the page. She'd read the damned thing multiple times, but she still found it impossible to comprehend. Looking up from her father's masculine handwriting Fallon scanned the room until her eyes locked with Cameron Barnes.

"You knew, didn't you?" She still couldn't say the words—speaking them aloud was more than she could grasp at the moment. "The day I talked to Lilly, you sat in that chair,"—she motioned to the wingback seat he was sitting in now, before continuing—"and you let me talk about how I'd struggled for years to get to a point where my grief didn't make the simple act of getting out of bed seemed like an insurmountable task. Yet you didn't say anything."

"I didn't know as much as you seem to think, Fallon. In my experience, speaking up before you have all the facts is as dangerous as keeping quiet. I'd hoped your father left an explanation in the puzzle, and he did." Cameron Barnes appeared unfazed by her anger, and if she was honest with herself, she'd admit her indignation was misplaced. He obviously sensed the shift because his expression softened. "I suspect it won't take much research to uncover Hagan Brody's connection to the people on that list. Personally, I doubt he is acting on his own. From what I've been able to learn, he is smart enough but highly unmotivated. Dealing with him will be easy, but you won't be truly safe until we find out who's calling the shots."

Fallon agreed. She considered Hagan moderately intelligent, but he was much too lazy to ever be successful without his family's help. His lack of motivation was one of the reasons she'd held a part of herself back when he'd insisted they were perfect for one another. She'd always felt disconnected from the relationship despite Hagan's relentless pursuit. Call it intuition, but something had always warned her there was something fundamentally wrong with the relationship.

The paper she'd been holding slowly slipped from her fingers as a soft caress along the side of her neck pulled Fallon back to the moment. Watching Carson read the letter she'd been holding as Silas wrapped her in his warm embrace, Fallon wasn't surprised when she heard Carson curse under his breath. The letter from her father included a detailed list of the people they'd investigated along with the location of the evidence gathered. When Carl handed her the puzzle's interior cylinder, Cameron had immediately moved to her side, citing the Agency's interest in the letter's contents. Before she'd finished reading, he'd already grabbed his phone and moved from the room. When he returned, she'd asked why he hadn't taken a picture of the list. He'd smiled and explained he'd only wanted to disclose the information relevant to the case.

Carson handed the letter to Silas before moving her into the circle of his arms while his friend read the letter. Fallon felt like she was watching everything from outside herself—the disconnection allowed her to take in the information without tumbling headfirst into the emotional storm lurking just under the surface. It was clear from her dad's letter he didn't think anyone knew their investigation was complete, but he'd been convinced most of the people they were watching wanted them out of the way before it went any further.

"I don't know what to do. It's overwhelming." The realization her life had once again been turned on end was making her head spin.

"Chef, take a breath, baby." Carson's words sounded a million miles away. In the distance, she heard Silas shout something about making her sit down, but the words were lost in the loud buzzing filling her ears. Looking on through the fog was quickly becoming more trouble than it was worth. Darkness beckoned, and the peace it offered was too much to resist.

CARSON WATCHED SILAS pull smelling salts from the cabinet in the club's first aid station and slip the small vial into his pocket. Calling the state-of-the-art medical room a station was an inside joke. The story among members was that while the brothers argued over how to furnish the room, Jax and Micah took over the project. The two men consulted a trauma specialist with experience treating BDSM medical issues and finished the entire area while their bosses were on their first mission as private contractors.

Silas's training as an EMT meant he'd been the one to sort through what the dungeon monitors called *a recovery kit* as Carson stood by silently seething with anger. Coming from a family where secrets were essentially impossible to keep, he didn't consider them an option, so it was hard for Carson to imagine anyone thinking the Fosters thought through this plan. Watching as she'd unrolled the letter,

Carson's attention shifted to Cam when he saw the man frown. When Barnes moved out of the room pressing numbers on his phone with more force than necessary, Carson stepped closer to the door so he could hear Cam's side of the conversation. He promised to forward a copy of the list as soon as possible, but Carson got the impression Cam was leaving out something significant. When he'd read the letter, Carson understood the hesitance he'd sensed. A tap on his shoulder made Carson turn to find Cam looking at him in concern. Nodding toward the hall, Cam moved out the door without watching to see if Carson followed.

"I'm going to go home to make a few calls. I think it's safe to say I'm not the first person Fallon will want to see when she comes fully awake." Carson had never seen Cam look as regretful as he did now. It was easy to see the man hated the difficult position he'd found himself in. "CeCe is going to be pissed when she gets wind of this mess. It'll be better if I talk to her before Tobi or Gracie get to her. Damn, this is a fucking train wreck. I can't believe this shit. I barely knew the Fosters, and I'm up to my ass in alligators in their mess."

Carson stared at the man for several seconds before shaking his head and laughing softly. "Man, I never thought I live to see the day a former spook would be worried about his wife hopping on the club gossip train."

"Fuck you, Carson. You're going to learn soon enough. Topping a smart woman is the best thing in the world. They learn the protocol quickly, and their intelligence makes earning their trust all the more precious—but having a sub who is brilliant and ambitious isn't easy. They are always thinking several steps ahead and see through a smokescreen before you have time to finish the story. And none of this takes into account their network of equally bright, well-connected network of friends."

Carson raised his hands in surrender, laughing because there was no doubt the man was speaking the truth, but it didn't change how he felt about Fallon. "She'll figure it out. I could see how overwhelmed she was, and you were the only person in the room who knew her parents." Carson pushed his fingers through his hair in frustration before sinking both hands into his front pockets. Rocking back on his heels, Carson grinned, "We'll talk to her, Cam. For the record, did you know what her dad set up?" The decision her parents made was so far beyond his comprehension, it was difficult for Carson to imagine.

"Not until a few hours ago. That's why I couldn't honestly deny the accusation I saw in her eyes. I probably should have suspected something was off earlier, but even though we were both employed by the Agency, we weren't close. I didn't know them well. We worked on different types of cases, so our paths rarely crossed." Cam was choosing his words carefully, and Carson understood the corner his friend had been painted into—and that it wasn't his own doing. "I will appreciate your help—God knows Carl isn't going to help. He's pissed as hell already. I looked at the letter even though he was adamant it was important for Fallon to have first dibs. I'm not going to apologize because it gave me a chance to get a little ahead of this thing."

"Meaning?" Carson knew Cam Barnes well enough to know if he said he'd gotten ahead of a situation, he had every piece of information available. He'd bet his sizable bank balance Cam already knew everything there was to know about the Fosters. One of the many things Carson admired about Cam was his resourcefulness. The man had contacts everywhere and could pull together information faster than any government on the planet.

"I found a couple living in a beach house in Aruba, I believe to be Fallon's parents." Carson should have been shocked by the revelation, but knowing Cam's ability to track down anyone no matter how hard they tried to hide—it wasn't as big a surprise as it should have been. "They've changed their names and had some minor facial surgery, but if I could find them, others will do the same. Cooper is on a plane as we speak. I want confirmation before taking the information to Fallon. I don't want her to suffer losing them again if this doesn't pan out."

"Thank you. The letter indicates they were planning to disappear, but she needs to know for sure one way or another." Carson wondered how much more Fallon could take. She'd weathered storm after storm, but even stone erodes when the wind and waves are relentless. Everyone has a breaking point, and he hoped like hell she would let them help. He and Silas couldn't change what had already happened, but they could help her sort through the emotional aftermath.

Once Cam turned to leave, Carson stepped back into the first aid station and felt his heart tighten in his chest. Fallon was sitting alone on the table, tears streaming down her pale cheeks. Silas was rifling through a medicine cabinet, chatting away, but it was clear she didn't hear a word. Carson couldn't remember the last time he'd seen anyone look so utterly lost. Moving to her side, Carson lifted her from the table before moving to a nearby chair. Settling her on his lap, he felt her stiffen before burying her face against his neck. Nearly silent sobs wracked her slender frame, the small sound drawing Silas's attention—*finally*.

"What happened? She was sitting on the table a few seconds ago." Filling a syringe, Silas moved to Fallon's side. Swabbing her arm, he held the thin barrel of the syringe where she could see it. "This is a mild sedative, Fallon. It won't make you sleep but will calm the storm enough you won't feel as though you've been strapped into a never-ending roller coaster." He waited for her to voice an objection. When she nodded, he quickly administered the sedative. Carson wasn't sure what Silas gave her or, but the effect was almost immediate. Whether the change was due to the medication or simply because she was expecting relief, Carson wasn't sure.

"I hope he gave you something good, girlfriend. Damn, you've been through the wringer." Tobi stood in the open doorway, looking at Fallon and shaking her head. "Lilly always tells me everyone is destined to have a certain number of challenges in their life. Some folks have all those bumps in the road spread out, and others seem to run into them like those damn rumble strips on the side of the freeway. Looks like you're racking up a lot of yours all at once, so you should have smooth sailing for many years after you power through this mess."

"Thanks. I hope you're right. Right now, it all feels like a strange dream where some elements feel real, and others are so outrageous you know they're nothing more than my imagination running wild."

"I'd be happy to call Lilly if you'd like to talk to her. I'm sure Kent and Kyle have called their dads, but as much as she may want to—I know she won't get into this unless you ask for her. As protective as she is, my mother-in-law respects the people she loves and tries to remember relationships have boundaries."

"Since when?" Kent's voice preceded his appearance.

Stepping from a hidden door at the side of the room, he looked at his wife and grinned.

"I'm going to throw you under the bus so fast you won't even see it coming. You have no idea how blessed you are to have Lilly West as a mother, and I'm not even going to mention how amazing your dads are. Boy, oh boy, you're going to be in so much trouble. You better start figuring out how you're going to make this up to your mama." Tobi's shift in direction served its purpose, and Carson was beginning to wonder if perfectly timed distractions were the woman's superpower. Fallon looked at her friend, and Carson could practically hear her unspoken questions.

"Silas gave me a small dose sedative. Before it levels me, I want to ask you a question." Tobi stepped closer, making certain Fallon knew she had the other woman's undivided attention. "As a parent, could you ever walk away from your children? Simply disappear, leaving behind a note saying call me after all the smoke clears?" To Tobi's credit, she didn't hesitate before pulling a chair so close she and Fallon were practically touching.

"There isn't anything in this world I wouldn't do to protect my kids. Don't get me wrong, Fallon, I don't agree with the way your parents handled this mess. I'm sure they assumed you would read the note long before now. They further assumed you'd know who to contact with the list, which seems like a huge leap since they hadn't leveled with you about what they were doing. It seems like they made a lot of assumptions and took chances I'd never consider, but honestly, I don't think any of us have enough information to judge them. Would I like to step between you and them to demand they answer a hundred and one questions? Damn straight. As your friend, I'd like to protect you from the pain, but I can't. What I can do is stand beside you, listen when you need to talk, and kick the ass of anyone you point out." By the time Tobi was finished, Fallon's eyes were shining with unshed tears, but Carson could feel the tension ebbing away from her.

"Thanks. I'd like to give the pool party another shot. Hopefully, Hagan will go back to New York as soon as he learns the list has been turned over to whoever gets that sort of thing. I'd like to enjoy those margaritas without looking over my shoulder the whole time." Fallon rubbed her forehead, trying to keep her mind focused, but Carson suspected she was losing the battle. "Knowing he only dated me to get to the puzzle should probably be humbling, but all I feel is relief. I'm happy to know I'm not a magnet for pricks."

"Me, too." Silas's murmured comment drew laughter from the men in the room.

"Another pool party it is. As soon as the dickless wonder you dated in New York goes home." Tobi gave Fallon a quick hug before whispering in a voice loud enough to be heard down the hall, "Your taste in men has improved exponentially since you moved to Texas. Carson and Silas are good men. They'll treat you right. You have friends here, Fallon—and we're keeping you." Carson was holding Fallon, so he wasn't able to give the vivacious blonde the hug she deserved, but Silas didn't miss the opportunity.

Silas thanked Tobi for her kind words and for her friendship. Feeling she was a part of a circle of friends would go a long way to ensure Fallon's happiness. Silas released Tobi to Kent, who leaned close, speaking low enough Carson couldn't hear what he was saying. Whatever Kent shared hadn't set well with Silas, his expression darkened as the two men moved into the hall. Carson looked down to see Fallon staring into space. Her eyes were open but unfocused. Whatever Silas gave her was hitting her harder than anyone expected.

"Come on, Chef. Let's go upstairs and get you something to eat before we kick back for a bit." He laughed to himself at the loopy grin she gave him.

"Can we make tacos? I heard Tex-Mex is different from the Mexican food in New York. I thought maybe there would be little mini tacos at the pool party since they had margaritas, but... oh, those drinks were so potent. Do you think there is any left? I would like to have some with the tacos. I'd like to get a look at the vial Silas used to see if I can still have a frozen margarita. Do you think the print is really small? If it's too small, I might not be able to read it until the drug wears off." She giggled like a schoolgirl before shrugging. "That seems silly, doesn't it? If I wait for my eyesight to focus, I won't need to read the label. Damn, why does everything always have to be a Catch-22?"

"I think it's safe to assume you shouldn't add alcohol to the mix." Carson made a quick call to his favorite Mexican food restaurant, ordering enough food to feed a small army. Promising the college students working the late shift a hefty bonus if they delivered the meal quickly, Carson bet they were at the gate in record time.

"You ordered food? That's so sweet. Why didn't you let me wear panties?" Jax McDonald snorted a laugh before letting Carson know he'd be accompanying them upstairs. Carson set Fallon on her feet, surprised when she remained steady. "Let's go upstairs. I'm hungry. Do you think we can make tacos?" Both men laughed as they led her the short distance to the elevator.

Chapter Twenty

"**Y**OU HAVE TO be fucking kidding me." Carson stared at Jax, completely flummoxed. It was almost impossible to believe anyone would have the balls to show up at the front gate of one of the most respected Special Ops teams in the world, spewing nonsense a third-grader could see through. Jax relayed the story to Carson as soon as Fallon excused herself to the restroom.

"I wanted to give you a heads-up before I talked to Fallon. No one is buying his story, but she has a right to know what's happening downstairs."

"What's wrong? I heard Carson cursing and my name." Carson turned his attention to the hall, surprised to see Fallon standing in the shadows. "The sedative might relax me, but it didn't render me stupid. It wasn't hard to figure out why Jax accompanied us upstairs—it was obvious he had something he wanted to tell you once I was out of the room. Just my damned luck he was facing the other way, and I only caught my name." Jax chuckled and shrugged.

"I swear this damned club is a magnet for brilliant women. As inconvenient as it is at times, it's also reassuring to know we're all kept on our toes." Fallon settled on one of the bar stools before returning her attention to Jax.

"Did Hagan do something stupid?" Jax frowned, and Fallon laughed. "Don't look so surprised. It wasn't much of a stretch. It's his… damn, what do the cops call it? Oh, yes.

It's his M.O. He isn't the brightest crayon in the box, Mr. McDonald."

"Jax. Please call me, Jax, unless we're in a club setting." She nodded her understanding, the movement so exaggerated she almost fell off the stool.

"Come on, Chef. Let's move to the sofa. If you're going to tumble to the floor, I'd prefer you were much lower." It only took Jax a couple of minutes to fill Fallon in on what was taking place downstairs.

"Jen? Beautiful, blonde, Jen? The woman whose legs go on forever? She's interrogating Hagan?" When Jax and Carson both chuckled, Fallon grinned. "Please tell me you are videotaping it. She is going to chew him up one side and down the other before she spits him out. She'll probably use big words—someone should be standing by to interpret for him."

"I didn't stick around for the interview but considering his ridiculous story about you stealing the puzzle from him. I'm looking forward to watching the video. Jen McCall is going to get into his head so quick he won't have time to admire the skin she's flashing." Jax rolled his eyes and laughed out loud. "Sam and Sage are going to blow a gasket. They hate it when she's the lead interrogator. She can paint a perp into a corner faster than anyone I've ever seen."

Carson watched the exchange between Fallon and Jax, shocked she seemed amused rather than angry the man she'd dated accused her of stealing the last gift her father had given her. Her attitude spoke volumes and made him grateful for the level of trust Fallon had shown in their relationship.

"Sam and Sage are Jen's husbands?" When Carson and

Jax both nodded, Fallon continued, "Sorry, I'm usually good with names and faces, but this whole thing has me off my game. I'm tired of everyone yanking the damned rug out from under me. I knew Brody and I didn't have a future together after the first date. This is what I get for not telling him to piss off when I should have. Who did you say was going to blow a gasket? Damn it, what did Silas give me? I'm a pharmacist, I should have asked. Holy hell, I'm always cautioning people against blindly taking meds without asking questions… and then—what did I do? The same damned thing. There isn't a hypocrite of the week award, is there? I'd win that sucker hands down and probably never live it down. Is it getting darker in here?"

Carson pulled Fallon against his side as her eyelids dropped. Watching the slow rise and fall of her chest, Carson shook his head. "She lasted longer than I thought she would."

"I don't know what Silas gave her, but I'm glad her mind is resting. Damn, she was spinning dangerously close to the edge." Carson agreed. It was obvious she'd been spinning and not in the way he and Silas preferred. "I know I'm preaching to the choir, but I'm going to say it, anyway. If you think she is the one you guys have been waiting for, you need to get her into your space as soon as possible. After tonight, it's a safe bet her ex is going to be headed back to New York with his tail between his legs. Screw whatever social conventions or timelines you think might apply." Carson appreciated Jax's advice. It was unnecessary but appreciated.

"Let me get her settled. See if you can find a couple of beers among the top-shelf liquor and expensive wine the Wests keep stocked in the bar." Returning a few minutes later, Carson grabbed the beer Jax thrust his way and led the way out to the deck.

"Her ex is a real piece of work. I used the remote link to look in on the interview. I have to tell you, I'm glad I'm not in the room—there's not a chance in hell I could keep a straight face. Jen is playing him like a song. She's amazing. I swear her neighbor in DC taught her well." Carson remembered hearing Jen had been friends with an older woman who lived in her apartment building. The woman was a retired spook who'd taken Jen under her wing. Jen swore she'd learned more by accident from her neighbor than she'd gotten from four years at an ivy league university.

Jax took a long, slow drink from the bottle in his hand before leaning against the rail. "I swear Jen's secret weapon is that no one sees her coming. They see the outside, and let's face it, the woman is model gorgeous. She plays the part and blindsides women as well as men."

"I haven't worked with her, but from what I've seen, she's never met a challenge she didn't master."

"True enough, but I have to tell you—the clothes she's almost wearing are enough to scramble Brody's brain. The video of this interview will be used for training until the end of time."

One Hour Earlier

KYLE LEANED BACK in his chair, watching the monitor in front of him as Hagan Brody stared with open-mouth wonder. The damned man's head swiveled on his shoulders so far, Kyle wondered how it kept from popping off his shoulders.

"How did you convince him to wait? I'm surprised he didn't insist on talking to one of us." Kent pulled a chair around so he could see the screen.

"The guys at the gate deserve a raise. They blew so much smoke up his ass it's a wonder it didn't come out of his ears. They fed him a line about the two of us being out of town. When he was led into the main room downstairs, they told him we'd left our Administrative Assistant in charge, and she was in the middle of a *session*."

"Session? What the hell is that supposed to mean?"

"You are not going to believe this shit. Sam is going to go out of his damned mind. Sage and Jen have outdone themselves this time." As he finished speaking, Jen McCall sauntered into the room wearing thigh-hugging black leather boots with spiked heels so high, Kyle had no idea how she walked in them. Her skirt was so short it barely qualified as clothing. Black fishnet stockings were secured on her upper thighs by a matching lace garter belt, leaving enough tanned skin exposed to tempt a saint. A barely-there black lace bra topped off an outfit most Dommes could only dream of pulling off.

"Holy fucking hell. Sam is going to kill Sage." Kyle could hear the amusement in his brother's voice but also knew Kent well enough to note the concern underlying the humor. Sage McCall was a wildcard on his best day, but this plan was a long way over the line the two brothers usually followed with their wife.

"What the fuck?" Sam McCall stood beside Kyle, staring at the screen. "I leave my idiot brother alone with our wife for one evening, and this happens? Somebody want to update me before I skin Sage alive?" Kyle repeated the story Fallon's ex-boyfriend fed the men stationed at the gate. "He claims she stole the cryptex from him. Fallon said she'd never told him it was a cryptex. She'd only said he'd given her a puzzle."

"So, he's working with someone here?" Kyle understood Sam's surprise. None of them wanted to think someone from the club was working with Brody.

"That's our best guess and the reason Jen is going to have a chat with him. Hell, from the look on his face, I think she could have gotten the information wearing jeans and a turtleneck." Kyle shook his head at the man's head spinning double-take when Jen entered the room. Watching her long legs eat up the space between them gave Brody plenty of time to take it all in. When the man started squirming in his chair, Jen tilted her head to the side in a move so subtle it was easy to miss, but it wasn't wasted on Brody. He'd interpreted the move as interest, falling face-first into the first of many body language traps Jen would set during the short interaction.

"She is going to eat him up and spit him out before he knows what hit him. If he wasn't staring at my wife's crotch, I'd almost feel sorry for the dumb bastard." Sam leaned back against the credenza behind Kyle's deck, crossed his ankles, and tapped the timer on his watch. "Ninety seconds, gentlemen. She'll have whatever she's after in less than a minute and a half—starting." He tapped his watch a second time as Jen used the flogger she was carrying to lift Brody's chin, so his eyes met her.

"My eyes are up here, Mr. Brody." Jen's sultry purr drew a curse from Sam as they watched the other man gulp. "I hear you believe one of our employees has something that belongs to you. Explain." When Hagen Brody's gaze dropped to Jen's breasts, she sighed and once again used the deer-skin flogger to lift his chin. "Maybe you should schedule a play session with a Mistress. A good flogging would do wonders for your concentration."

"Honey, my focus is exactly where I want it to be." Jen smiled, not giving any indication she'd found the comment disrespectful.

"Tell me why you believe something belonging to you is at Prairie Winds. With the Wests out of town, I'm in charge." Jen lifted herself up onto the table next to the one where Brody sat. With an exaggerated movement, she spread her legs just enough to extend one more than the other as she crossed her legs in a move so blatantly sexual it was almost obscene.

"Christ, the woman is racking up punishment points at a record pace—and that's saying a lot because her top speed is nothing to sneeze at." Kent and Kyle both chuckled at Sam's comment because neither doubted him for a second.

"Hagen—it's okay if I call you Hagen, isn't it?" Without waiting for him to respond, she leaned forward, giving him a bird's eye view of her barely covered breasts. "What makes you think we have something that belongs to you?"

"Not you. Well, not you, specifically. Fallon Foster stole a cryptex from me when I broke up with her. She took off for Texas before I realized she'd taken it. I met a woman who told me Fallon works here and that she bragged about the puzzle."

"You met a woman? Where?"

"At a café up the road. Amazing coincidence, really." Everything about the man's body language screamed he was lying, and Kyle knew from Jen's expression she hadn't missed the tells.

"What makes you think this woman knows what she is talking about?" Jen's inquiry should have been a red flag for the man. I probably would have made him think twice if any of his blood was making its way to his brain. From the way he shifted in his seat, it was safe to say Jen crossing her arms, pushing her breast so high they were perilously close to spilling out of her bra, had stolen his ability to think clearly.

"I swear I'd shoot the asshole myself if I didn't understand what he's going through. She pulls that shit with me, and I'm toast every damned time." Kyle laughed at Sam's comment, understanding too well. Tobi had been known to play on the edge as well—and when she did, it was impossible to resist. Jen McCall always had the confidence to pull off something like this, but Kent and Kyle's wife, Tobi, was a different story. Knowing he and his brother played a large part in Tobi's confidence was one of the things in Kyle's life that he was most proud of.

Jen leaned close to Brody, whispering something so low even the state-of-the-art sound system wasn't able to pick up the words. Whatever she said made the man nod furiously before he spoke so fast Kyle almost missed the most important piece of information. *Nancy Dressler*. The woman became a problem soon after joining the club.

"I should have ended her membership as soon as I discovered she'd withheld the fact she knew a club member." Knowing a club member prior to joining wasn't a problem—hell, it was usually a benefit. What he'd found problematic and more than a little questionable was the way she'd denied having met Carson Scott despite them hailing from the same small town nestled along the eastern border of Texas.

Before Kyle could comment, his phone pinged with an incoming message. Silas was pretending to work behind the bar, polishing everything in sight and moving around the space with a clipboard. To make certain Jen was safe, he'd insisted on being close, knowing Sam or Sage would likely tip their hand with body language alone. There was no way either of them could watch the vixen they'd married pull this off without growling at Hagen Brody.

Making sure you caught the name of the inside source. Alert Carson..

Kyle let Silas know they were on it. He'd already electronically deactivated the woman's gate pass, and she'd be served paperwork within the hour letting her know she was no longer a club member. While it was rare for them to take such a hardline on a first offense, endangering not only a new member and employee but several others as well was inexcusable. Kyle delayed the call to Carson until after Jen sent Brody on his way. He didn't want to miss any of their interaction. Jen was trained and more than capable of disabling the man sitting in front of her, but that didn't mean Kyle was leaving anything to chance.

"Let me tell you a secret, Mr. Brody. No one here is buying your story. I have it on good authority the puzzle in question has already been opened. The contents were handed over to authorities a couple of hours ago. Your best bet is to hightail it back to New York and cover your ass. Whoever sent you here will probably be less than pleased with your sub-par performance. If I had to guess, I'd put my money on it being the norm for you, but I don't care enough about your sex life to make inquiries."

With a flick of her wrist, Jen gave the man's thigh a lash he would have certainly felt through his designer slacks. Hagen Brody yelped and jumped to his feet, cursing. His foul language didn't intimidate Jen—in fact, she found it amusing, her hearty laugh drawing a frown from Brody.

"You're a bitch. Some man needs to teach you a lesson." Brody snarled the words through clenched teeth, but Jen simply rolled her eyes.

"Maybe so, but it won't be you. Be gone before I kick your ass just for practice." As Jen turned to walk away, Hagen Brody made the mistake of moving a fraction of a second too soon. Jen caught the motion in her peripheral vision and sent the man to his knees with a single kick.

"Damn, I bet that hurt like a *bitch*, didn't it?" Jen's response made Sam lean his head back and laugh.

"Brody said the one thing guaranteed to push her over the edge. Being called a bitch straight up pisses Jen off. Damn, that was fun to watch." Sam was still chuckling as he moved toward the door. "I better get down there before she sends him to the hospital. If he's stupid enough to say it again, she'll make sure he will never be able to reproduce." Sam paused, looking as though he was considering whether or not that was really a problem before grasping the door handle. "It would likely be for the greater good, but some things are best left to karma."

Chapter Twenty-One

Two Days Later

F ALLON WIPED TEARS from her eyes and held her
stomach. She couldn't remember the last time she'd
laughed so hard. If she hadn't already asked to have the
video rewound twice, she'd ask again. Watching Jen
McCall drop Hagen to his knees with a well-placed kick
was the best thing she'd seen in years. Seeing him fall
forward, face-planting two seconds later was icing on the
cake. Taking a sip from the enormous margarita she held in
her hand, Jen gave a negligent shrug. They'd taken advantage of Silas and Carson's well-stocked bar, and the
generous platters of snacks their housekeeper whipped up
on short notice.

"He called me a bitch and then iced it by making a
move I caught out of the corner of my eye. He should
consider himself lucky because Silas was already vaulting
himself over the bar. I still want to know how he pulled
that off—it was like he was on springs." The women
gathered around all laughed as they toasted Silas for his
impressive kangaroo hop over the chest-high bar. "Unfortunately, all the cameras were pointed in the same
direction, so I'm the only one who saw it." Jen raised her
glass, looking around the room for the cameras she was
sure had been set up for the group's impromptu party,

"Here's to you, Silas. I may be the only witness to your amazing leap, but I promise to share the story of your athletic prowess at every *hopportunity*."

Groans erupted from the group celebrating Jen's takedown of Hagen Brody as well as the men watching the video feed. Fallon had only been here two days, but she knew several things in the men's family room had been rearranged while she'd dressed for the party. No doubt the décor changes were to made to accommodate cameras and microphones, but none of her guests seemed to care. Fallon didn't fully understand the Doms' obsessive need to monitor their submissives. When she'd said as much, Tobi blushed as several others laughed.

"Don't pay any attention to them. They blame me for the over-the-top security measures, but I'm not the only one who seems to attract trouble without really trying." Tobi turned to glare at Jen, whose faux look of innocence was enough to bring gales of laughter from the group.

"Before everyone gets mired in the blame-game quagmire, I want to ask Fallon if we're still on for tomorrow. I'm looking forward to showing you where we are on the pharmacy project and getting your input before all the final plans are made. I know you only moved in a couple of days ago, and I hate rushing you…"

"But you're going to do it, anyway. Really CeCe, you might as well drop the façade of patience. We're two peas in a pod. We can't pull off phony to save our souls." CeCe stared at Lilly West for several seconds before her shoulders dropped in defeat.

"True enough. I keep thinking I'll turn over a new leaf and morph into Little Miss Polly Patience, but my guardian angel is always putting out fires and never seems to have time to draw up a new plan."

"Honey, you stay just the way you are. You're a hero to children and their parents." Lilly's expression switched from compassion to mischief between one breath and the next. "Besides, if you change, I'll be left as the only one who's seen as openly demanding. You don't want to do that to me, do you?"

"No pressure there, CeCe." Gracie had been quiet until Lilly spread the guilt on extra thick. She loved the woman like a second mother and recognized the ploy. Hell, she'd seen the older woman use the same routine on Tobi a time or two.

"Remember the time Lilly tried to talk me into having another baby? Holy hell, she pulled every rabbit in Texas out of her hat." Tobi leaned back, laughing as she thought back on one of the few times she'd actively avoided her mother-in-law.

"A couple of weekends spent babysitting the dynamic duo cured her of that notion." Gracie giggled when Lilly threw a pillow at her. "Admit it, those two were a handful. You, of all people, should have understood what it was like having twins."

"Of, I understood. But I wanted to be Wonder Granny, and I figured my odds would improve if more children were involved." Letting out a dramatic sigh, Lilly's entire face lit up as she laughed. "Damn, those two kicked my ass when I kept them. I'd no sooner get one out of a mess and cleaned up than I'd have to catch up with the other and start the whole process again. Del and Dean always seemed to have pressing business in Houston whenever the kids were staying over. Highly suspicious, but I could never prove Kent or Kyle were giving them a heads up."

Fallon looked on as the group continued to banter back and forth, suddenly realizing how much she'd missed growing up with parents where the only constant was their inconsistency. Now they'd left her in an almost impossible position. Knowing they'd walked away from her without looking back went against everything she'd believed about her parents. Cherished memories she'd held close to her heart since she lost them were tainted with what seemed like the ultimate betrayal. Taking a deep breath, Fallon refocused on the here and now.

Looking around the open space, Fallon was surprised at how comfortable she felt in Silas and Carson's home. They insisted it was her home as well, but until she could contribute financially, Fallon knew she wouldn't feel one hundred percent at home. By the time her new friends had all been escorted to their cars and were all on their way home, Fallon was, once again, knee-deep in overthinking every detail of the past few years.

How many other people in her life had been sent to retrieve what her dad gave her? Had there been people watching them in the café when her dad gave her the puzzle? Did he realize she'd be targeted, or did he assume she'd open the damned thing immediately and turn the information over to authorities? Why push the responsibility over to her? Was she so expendable he didn't care about painting a target on her back? After graduating from high school, her parents had both become oddly distant, but she'd assumed they were trying to make her independent. Now she wondered if there wasn't something else behind the shift.

"Sweetheart, I don't know where your mind has gone, but we need you to come back to us." Silas's smooth voice lured her out of the melancholy mind-space she'd been wandering around in. "We need to talk to you about the letter. Have you decided what you want to do?"

"You can take your time, Chef. Nothing says you have to decide right away." Carson's assurance helped her relax. Fallon hadn't realized how much pressure she was putting on herself to make a decision.

"Why would they walk away and leave me holding the bag? I didn't know what they were into, and this is one case where ignorance is definitely not bliss." Pausing to gather her thoughts, Fallon stared at her lap, willing her fingers to unclench. Pulling in a deep breath, she looked up to see the concerned looks on Silas and Carson's faces. "I know I could do this without you, but... well, I don't want to." Huge smiles spread over their faces; the change made them look like the carefree boys she suspected they'd been while growing up. One grew up in the mountains, basically raised by the entire community, while the other was raised by an extended family in the bayous of coastal Texas and Louisiana.

"We've waited so long for you, Chef. Knowing you are making the choice to let us help is huge."

"Carson is right. It's one thing to admit you need help—and I want to make it perfectly clear we never want you to hesitate to ask for our assistance, but it's next level to know you are capable of handling a situation but know we can make the process easier. Some Dominants want to micromanage their submissive's lives, but we prefer to manage our play while partnering with you in life." Fallon's eyes filled with tears as she listened to Silas describe the kind of relationship she'd always dreamed of having.

"We've never wanted a twenty-four-seven slave. Someone who mindlessly follows every command with no thought for their own needs holds no appeal." Silas pulled her hands into his as he spoke. It was a small act but felt so intimate she could practically feel the connection between them strengthening. Fallon felt the same link with Carson and wondered why it happened so quickly. Maybe it was something she could talk to CeCe about tomorrow while they toured the pharmacy construction site.

"Mindlessly following orders isn't going to happen. I was a well-behaved kid, and look where it got me." As an only child, Fallon didn't have the luxury of blaming a sibling if a chore wasn't done or something was broken. She'd always rolled her eyes when people assumed she was spoiled simply because she didn't hail from a large family. For her being an only child meant your parents only had one kid to watch, so they didn't miss even the smallest infraction.

"Remember, our focus is on your safety, pleasure, and happiness. Everything we do will be with those things in mind. Until we know each other better, we'll depend on the stoplight system during scenes. Outside of D/s play, communication is still paramount. If you have a bad day, we want to hear about it." When they first met, she'd assumed Carson was the stricter of the two, but she was seeing a different side of him the more time they spent together.

"If you are concerned about someone or something, we want you to feel comfortable enough to come to us with whatever is bothering you. We'll do our best to listen without trying to solve every problem, something I have heard our female friends complain about too often to count." Silas grinned, and Fallon nodded in agreement because she'd heard friends and coworkers make the same observation.

"I'm meeting CeCe at the pharmacy site first thing in

the morning. If one of you could give me a ride, I'd appreciate it. She said it wasn't far and offered to give me a ride back after we finished." The men frowned at each other, making her wonder what she'd said wrong.

"I'll be able to take you. Carson has an early staff meeting tomorrow. If CeCe can't drive you back here, ask her to call me, and I'll pick you up. She's right, it isn't fair, but we haven't been able to confirm Brody has left the state." Fallon was sure he'd have left as soon as he found out she no longer had the contents of the puzzle. In some ways, it was a pity he'd left before she had the chance to tell him exactly what she thought of him. Giving a mental shrug, she knew it wouldn't make any difference to him, but damn, it would feel great to unload some of her anger on one of the people who deserved it.

"As far as my parents. I'm going to take some time and think about whether or not I want to contact them. I haven't asked, but I bet someone in the Prairie Winds group has already checked out the phone number in the letter." Silas and Carson's expressions never changed. Damn, they had the best poker faces she'd ever seen. She might feel ambivalent about contacting her parents after the way they'd abandoned her, but she was confident the men in front of her and their friends were already tracking down the elusive pair. "I'll bet the number is no longer in service. Who knows where they finally landed?" The only change she saw was a slight tightening of Carson's jaw. "I'm right, aren't I? I don't know Cameron Barnes well, but I'll wager a steak dinner he's already put his nose to the ground like a bloodhound determined to track them down. If he's found someone matching their description, he's sent someone to check."

"I love smart women, but it's damned hard to keep

anything from them." Silas chuckled as he shook his head.

"I didn't need to be smart to figure it out. Mr. Barnes strikes me as a man who doesn't like being out of the loop." Both men laughed out loud, letting Fallon know she was right.

"That's an understatement, Sweetheart. Cam's been accused of being an information junkie. Personally, I think that's a bit harsh, but I'd certainly agree he is an information sponge. Cam takes the old saying *'Information is power'* seriously—very, very seriously." Silas's comment made perfect sense considering the man's former profession.

"I don't know anybody who begrudges Cam's thirst for knowledge. Hell, he's saved several members' asses because he was able to get information no one else could. He's an amazing resource, and you're right to assume he is making a lot of inquiries on your behalf." Carson's admission wasn't a surprise, but it still felt odd that so many people she'd known such a short time were going to extraordinary measures to help her.

"It's humbling and overwhelming." Fallon hadn't intended to say the words out loud, but the shift in their expressions assured her she had.

"Having friends who help?" Silas correctly guessed where her thoughts had gone. Both men seemed tuned into her thinking, making her wonder how long it would take her to anticipate their needs as well. Perhaps this was another question for CeCe, or maybe she'd wait until their pool party re-do. Several of the ladies were in polyamorous marriages and might be willing to offer guidance... and if she caught them before their second margarita, the answers might even be coherent.

FALLON FOLLOWED CECE through the construction site between the building currently used as a clinic and the much larger structure housing the pediatric orthopedic hospital. The architects designing the pharmacy did a phenomenal job utilizing the enormous courtyard without stealing every inch of the outdoor space. "Your use of the space maximizes its potential in a way that's unusual unless the designers have personal experience."

"I'd like to say they were inspired, but it's more likely they're terrified of Cam. He oversaw a few of the design meetings because I was tied up in surgery. I swear children love him, but adults shake in their boots when he starts asking them questions. Our kids and those of our friends have his number big time, but my staff scatters when he shows up. Hell, I saw a male sub pee his pants because he thought Kyle was going to hand him over to Cam for a punishment."

Fallon's face must have reflected the fear gripping her at the thought of being turned over to another Dom. It probably meant something for her to be terrified of being touched by anyone other than Carson or Silas, but she was too lost in fear to figure it out.

"Good heavens, every ounce of color just drained from your face. Your men aren't ever going to let anyone else touch you. Any Dom who tried to put their hands on me would probably pull back a stump. And no one touches Tobi, Gracie, or Jen but their men. The sub I was talking about was a trainee. He'd filled out all the forms, listed his hard and soft limits." Fallon was still trying to reconcile the BDSM play she'd read about and the real-life interactions.

"Damn, girl, take a breath. Silas and Carson will pitch a fit if you pass out and get hurt. It won't do much for my reputation as a physician either, but I can play that off because you're a big person. Little people are my special-ty." Fallon appreciated CeCe making light of her over-reaction. Now was a good time to ask some questions she'd been holding back during their tour.

An hour later, Fallon had accepted the job CeCe of-fered, contingent on her license being successfully transferred. CeCe assured her it was a slam dunk, citing help Fallon was getting from club members. The famous surgeon had also been a font of information about poly relationships, assuring Fallon it was common for the bonds to form very quickly. By the time CeCe's emergency pager started shrieking, they'd both had enough coffee to keep them awake for hours. As she ran down the hall toward the hospital, CeCe shouted an apology over her shoulder for not being able to drive Fallon home.

It wasn't until Fallon stepped outside that she realized Carson and Silas hadn't returned her phone. Looking around, she didn't see anyone she knew, then rolled her eyes at her own absurdity. The chances of her knowing anyone walking by were so small it was laughable. It was already warming up, so she didn't want to wait around for Silas or Carson to notice she hadn't returned. The drive-way for their house was less than a mile, so she decided her best bet was to walk.

Chapter Twenty-Two

WATCHING FALLON FOSTER walk out of the construction area between Dr. Cecelia Barnes' clinic and the surgical hospital could only mean one thing—the bitch was planning to stay in Texas. Nancy seethed as the woman who'd upended all her plans walked toward the busy street. "I was on track to make Carson Scott my own. Damn it, I was even willing to deal with his New Age Hippy roommate... well, for a while anyway." Her plan was to start a family as soon as possible to cement her place with Carson, then find a way to send Silas packing.

Carson had been raised in a close-knit family that included many extended members. There was no way he'd ever walk away from her if she had his baby. Her carefully laid plans were nuked last night when she'd been notified her membership to Prairie Winds was revoked. Kent and Kyle West hadn't been obligated to refund the unused portion of her membership fee, but they'd included a certified check with the hand-delivered message.

Nancy had saved for over a year to afford the outrageous cost of joining the club. It had taken her several weeks to get Carson's attention and even longer to time everything right, so she was the submissive he and Silas chose for a scene. Nancy read everything she could find on submission, practicing the various poses until she could complete the moves required with flawless grace. The men had complimented her during every phase of their scene, and at the end of the night, they kissed her, promising to see her again soon. She'd shared a few brief encounters over the next couple of months, but nothing significant enough to seal the deal.

Since Fallon Foster's arrival, neither Carson nor Silas had even spoken to her. When she'd secured an invitation to the pool party Tobi West hosted for Fallon, Nancy tried to connect with Carson. She'd only been a few feet from him when that damned drone ruined everything. When she met Hagen Brody and learned he'd been the one operating the aerial device that foiled her plan, she'd wanted to smack the arrogant bastard upside the head. It wasn't until he offered her money and assured her Carson would walk away from Fallon if Nancy helped him find the puzzle his ex stole from him before moving to Texas that she agreed to answer his questions.

Nancy held back until Fallon made her way to the sidewalk. Letting her get a half-a-block head start, Nancy was pleased to see the other woman was walking close to the edge of the road. All Nancy would need to do was claim she swerved to miss an animal darting across the road. Speeding up as she rounded the corner onto the road, Nancy was so focused on her target, she didn't see the Hummer bearing down on her.

"DIDN'T YOU TELL me Nancy Dressler threw Fallon under the bus with that Brody fellow, and the boys kicked her out of the club?" Lilly looked across the front seat at Tobi as she merged onto the busy road.

"Yes, why?"

"She was sitting at a stop sign back there watching Fallon walk down the road, and she didn't look happy." The car Nancy was driving passed them, but Tobi caught up easily. "That crazy bitch is going to hit Fallon." Tobi could hear the alarm in Lilly's voice. Her mother-in-law was usually unflappable. If Lilly West was scared, things were definitely going to hell, so Tobi didn't hesitate to press the panic alarm on her bracelet. Hitting the gas, it took little effort for her heavy vehicle to send Nancy's lightweight Kia skidding off the road before the small car clipped Fallon.

The impact pushed the lightweight vehicle onto the shoulder of the road but hadn't been enough to roll it into the ditch. Skidding to a stop, Tobi motioned for Fallon to get in when she spun around to check out the commotion behind her. Fallon scrambled into the car, her face pale as she realized how close she'd come to being hit.

"Damn, Texas is dangerous. I already got nailed by the mirror on Silas's truck. Now, this? Do you think the driver was trying to hurt me deliberately?" Nancy Dressler got out of her car, zeroed in on the Hummer, and stomped closer.

"This is going to be fun. She can't see us because of the tinted windows." Lilly rubbed her hands together in anticipation before picking up her phone and hitting the record button on the camera.

"Are you fucking stupid?" Nancy screeched as she approached the passenger's side. Tobi had already phoned emergency services and was dialing Kyle when his Lexus roared into view. "What the fucking hell? Who the hell do you think—" She stopped abruptly when Lilly rolled her window the rest of the way down and turned to face her.

Tobi had no idea how Kent and Kyle closed the distance between their car and hers so quickly, but the next voice she heard was Kyle's, "Step away from the car, Ms. Dressler. I'd advise you to be very careful how you speak to my wife and mother. Until we find out what's happened here, you'd be wise to tread carefully."

"Your crazy wife shouldn't be allowed to drive. She bumped me off the road. I'm calling the police." She'd no sooner spoken the words than the sound of approaching sirens filled the air.

"Already taken care of." Kent opened Tobi's door to lean in and pull her into a bone-crushing hug. "You okay? I swear my heart skips several beats every time your alarm sounds, but damn, I'm glad you have it."

"Nancy was going to hit Fallon. She was driving straight for her. I bumped her off the road before she got close enough. I'm sorry about the Hummer." Tobi looked down to see her hands shaking so hard she was forced to press them together.

"We don't care about the Hummer, sweetness. The only thing that matters is the three of you are okay. Stay inside until we deal with Ms. Dressler and the police. You'll have to make statements, but we'll set those up for after you've regrouped."

He pulled her dash-cam from its bracket and grinned. "We'll make sure Parker gets this." As the top-ranking law enforcement officer for their area, long-time club member Parker Andrews would make the final call concerning the incident. Tobi was relieved to know it would be in his capable hands despite her concern it would be impossible to prove what she'd instinctively known.

"But you don't know what's on it? What if it makes me look like a lunatic?" Tobi knew what Nancy had planned but worried she wouldn't have any way to prove it.

"We've already seen the footage, Kitten." Tobi listened

as Kyle spoke from his mother's side, her trembling fingers wrapped in his large hand. "We can remote into the camera, and we did as soon as you pressed your panic alarm." His eyes softened as he glanced at her trembling hands clutched tightly in her lap. "Thank you for activating your alarm so quickly. Knowing that was your first reaction means more to us than we can possibly say."

Kyle's words went straight to her heart, and Tobi felt herself relax. Before she could respond, both back doors opened at the same time. Silas slid in behind her as Carson moved into the seat behind Lilly. Fallon squeaked as the men pressed her between them.

"Sweetness, are you okay?" Tobi wasn't surprised to hear the concern in Silas's voice. She knew the two men had been waiting for a long time to find a woman to share. He'd told her a few months ago they were getting close to giving up. She'd encouraged him to hang in there, assuring him blessings always seem to show up when you least expect them. She was looking forward to reminding him about their conversation.

Tobi couldn't hear Fallon's reply but whatever she'd said drew a litany of curses from Carson. He gave her another quick hug before getting back out of the car. "I'll be right back. I'm going to have a chat with Nancy, then I'm going to make a couple of calls." Tobi looked at Kent in question, and he grinned.

"I'm sure Carson has plenty to say to Ms. Dressler. When he's finished making calls, she won't find a job anywhere but the bayou. She'll be on her way back home within the hour unless Fallon plans to press charges." Tobi understood why Fallon was reluctant to push the issue, even if Nancy deserved to spend time behind bars.

Once they'd been cleared to leave, Tobi was relieved

when Lilly opted to ride home with Del, who'd arrived shortly after Silas and Carson. Kyle moved her into his car, and Kent drove hers back to Prairie Winds, where they'd all agreed to meet. Carson led Fallon to his car while Silas hurried down the opposite side of the road to his truck. Tobi heard the two men promise Kyle they would drive Fallon to Prairie Winds after she'd calmed down.

Smiling to herself, Tobi knew what they meant. Carson and Silas needed a few minutes alone with Fallon. Kent and Kyle were usually the same—the time alone gave them a chance to reassure themselves she was alright. Tobi found the Doms' softer sides endearing but kept the observation to herself.

Kyle lifted her hand to his lips and kissed her trembling fingers as they drove to the club. "I'm so proud of you, Kitten. You made a split-second decision when others would have hesitated. Your quick thinking saved your friend. Fallon would have been seriously injured or worse if she'd been struck by Nancy's car."

"I wouldn't have known she was the one driving the car if your mom hadn't seen her. Today was certainly a team effort." Tobi took a deep breath, trying to calm her racing heart. "What will happen to Nancy?" She was angry at the younger woman but hated the thought of so many people she cared about being embroiled in a court case.

"She'll be out of town within hours. I don't know Fallon well enough to guarantee she won't press charges, but I can't see it happening. It seems more likely she'll want to put it all behind her."

"Fallon's life has been turned on end so many times, she must feel like she's never going to get her feet back under her." Tobi took a deep breath, remembering exactly what it felt like when your world was flipped end for end so many times you couldn't remember which way was up. "I hope she doesn't decide Texas is full of lunatics and make a run for it." Kyle glanced her way as he turned off the highway, his expression softer than it had been a few seconds earlier. Driving through the open gates, he slowed the car and smiled.

"Silas and Carson will convince her to stay, Kitten. Those two won't let her get away. The two of them waited for the right woman to walk into their lives, just as Kent and I did. It hasn't escaped my attention how much we have in common—although I didn't actually hit you with my truck."

"Only because I moved. I suspect there have been times you wished you could get another shot at me, but I'm older and wiser. I would stand to the side this time."

"Indeed, you are wiser. I can't tell you how grateful I am you pressed your alarm. There have been times we've wondered if you'd forgotten you had it." He parked the sleek, black car in the garage but didn't get out. Pulling her across the console and onto his lap, Kyle used the tips of his fingers to push a stray lock of hair behind her ear. "I haven't seen my mom that rattled for a long time. At first, I thought it was because you'd pushed Nancy's car aside."

"I don't think that's it. She has taken Fallon under her wing and seeing her targeted made her realize how difficult it is to protect the people you love. It was probably a humbling reminder of how challenging it was for her while you and Kent were in the Special Forces." Tobi pressed her cheek against his shoulder, relaxing against his muscular chest. "She told me those were the hardest years of her entire life. Knowing you were in some god-forsaken place, facing things she could barely imagine—and there wasn't anything she could do to protect you."

"It was hard enough letting our kids attend school in another city. I can't imagine letting them leave the state or, heaven forbid, the country. It's humbling to realize how strong my parents were to put up with everything we put them through, but I'll deny saying it if you tell them." Tobi couldn't hold back her giggle. This was the Kyle few people saw. He was so much more playful and wittier than most people knew. A part of her was thrilled it was a side of himself he didn't share with outsiders, but another part was often frustrated with other people's one-dimensional view.

By the time Silas and Carson escorted Fallon through the club's back doors, the impromptu party was in full swing. Tobi bumped Gracie's hip with her own and grinned. "I'm proud of us. We can put together a shindig faster than Clark Kent changes into his leotard."

"I think Superman might take offense at you referring to his superhero ensemble as a leotard." Gracie was Tobi's best friend, business partner, and often the one pulling her back when her plans went off the rails—which was more often than not. "Fallon fits between them perfectly." Gracie's observation mirrored Tobi's. Silas and Carson only left Fallon's side to bring her food, drinks or take one of the many phone calls they'd answered.

"Kent told me Fallon's agreed to run the pharmacy CeCe is building. When I had lunch with her last week, she said it was nearly complete. They were waiting on fixtures and someone to configure everything." Tobi teased CeCe about waiting, that it wasn't the ambitious woman's usual way of doing things.

"I know it seems out of character for her, but she asked me a few months ago how we learned to delegate. She was determined to turn over more of the business end of her practice so she could concentrate on being a doctor. CeCe said she'd hadn't realized how much of her time was spent managing the business end of things until she started planning their vacation." Tobi must have looked as confused as she felt because Gracie laughed. "I didn't get it either. CeCe said she had no trouble finding people to cover her medical appointments, but finding help with the business was torture. It showed her how much easier her life would be if she had managers for the various aspects of her business."

"We haven't known Fallon for very long, but you and I always seemed to agree when it came to quality people."

"And Fallon is a great choice for the pharmacy. She's young and driven." Tobi understood what Gracie was saying and agreed. In many ways, Fallon reminded Tobi of a younger version of CeCe. *Okay, maybe Kyle is right. She and I seem to have a lot in common.* "She reminds me of you. Smart as a whip… Brave enough to grab what she wants with both hands and hold on no matter how rough the ride gets."

Tobi was shocked by her friend's assessment. She and Gracie loved one another like sisters, but they rarely talked about their troubled pasts. To know the other woman held her in such high regard was humbling.

"Come on, let's go rescue Fallon. She needs some girl-time before her men steal her away."

"Insatiable. Damn, did you see her when they walked in? That girl is getting some knock your socks off sex. I'd be jealous if I wasn't getting my own."

"You know what I think?" Tobi felt the familiar tingle she got any time an idea was rolling around in her head. "We've been playing it safe entirely too long. Damn and double damn. We've completely destroyed our trouble-maker reputations."

"What?" Gracie's horrified response drew stares from some people closest to them. When Gracie simply smiled, they quickly returned to their conversations. "I can't believe you would say something so hateful. You make us sound like a couple of senior citizens."

"Hey, don't knock seniors. We've lived long enough to earn the right to ignore rules." Lilly stepped close and whispered, "Please tell me the two of you are plotting. I've had about all of this *well-behaved* nonsense I can stomach." Tobi and Gracie both laughed, but it was Gracie who answered.

"We were just discussing that very thing. I have no idea who this happened. It's mortifying to think we've dropped the ball in such a depressing manner." Lilly's solemn nod was all the encouragement Tobi needed.

"Let's go. We've got a new friend to corrupt."

Epilogue

Eight Months Later

FALLON WAS DEAD on her feet. She'd worked two shifts because one of her coworkers was still on family leave after his wife gave birth a few weeks ago, and the other missed her flight after attending a wedding in Hawaii. Fallon collapsed into her office chair and sighed.' She had a brief vision of herself leaning back in a cushioned lounge chair, watching the ocean waves lap against the shore. Closing her eyes, Fallon pictured herself ordering one of those fruity drinks with a tiny paper umbrella perched on the sugared edge of the glass. Maybe she'd make a spa appointment and get a massage. "I could really use a massage." She'd meant to say the words to herself, but when the pharmacy tech standing a few feet away giggled, Fallon knew she'd spoken out loud."

"Fallon, you need to go home. All the scripts are filled. I can wait for them to be picked up." The young woman was slated to graduate at the end of the current semester. If she passed her state board exams, Fallon planned to hire her. CeCe had only overseen the pharmacy for the first few months before turning management over to Fallon. Looking at the younger woman, Fallon appreciated all her hard work. She worked long hours to keep from starting her career buried under a mountain of student loan debt and was still graduating in the top five percent of her class.

Bristol Johnson also worked as a member of the club's cleaning crew. When Fallon asked if she planned to give up the job that kept her up until dawn three times a week, Bristol blushed and shook her head. "I can't afford the club's membership fees unless I keep working. I checked out two kink clubs in Dallas, and they weren't for me. There wasn't any screening process, and when I asked about the club's safe word, people looked at me like I'd grown a second head. It made me appreciate everything Prairie Winds does to make sure their members are safe."

Fallon nodded in agreement. She'd never visited any other BDSM clubs, but she'd heard horror stories from several people when she'd lived in New York. Bristol's upbeat personality and work ethic made her popular with her coworkers and the small pharmacy's customers. Fallon was looking forward to having an additional pharmacist on staff. The small facility she'd help set up was already bursting at the seams. CeCe was already talking to architects about ways to expand but knew their current staff couldn't be stretched much further.

"Silas called while you were talking to Benny's mother." Bristol grinned because she'd given up trying to explain the medication timeline to the little boy's shell-shocked mother and gratefully handed the exhausted woman over to Fallon. After sitting in the waiting room for ten hours worrying about her daredevil son's arm being pieced back together, his mom had barely been able to put one foot in front of the other. Tracking the complicated instructions for his medications had been so overwhelming she'd finally broken down. After a few calls, Fallon arranged for one of the off-duty pharmacy techs living in the same apartment complex to check on the patient and his stressed-out mother for the first forty-eight hours. She wanted to make certain the little fellow was getting his medication on time, and it was being properly administered.

"Are you listening to me, Fallon? Silas wanted to remind you they'd be waiting for you outside the front entrance after work." Fallon blinked several times, trying to refocus on what the other woman was saying.

"Damn, I forgot they drove me to work. I better get moving. Thanks for all your help today. I swear you can tell when it's a full moon. Sports injuries skyrocket, and the parents all look like they've been run over by a loaded truck. The medical staff schedules extra people, but it never seems to be enough." Another wave of fatigue hit her, and she sent up a silent prayer she wasn't coming down with something. Fallon had been surprised how quickly she'd adjusted to the warmer climate.

Silas and Carson recently accompanied her on a quick trip to New York to finalize some paperwork related to her parents' phony death certificates. The short business trip was a stark reminder of how brutally cold it was in New York during the winter. The trip also served as a torturous reminder she still hadn't decided about contacting her parents. Silas and Carson regularly reminded her there was no reason to rush a decision. Their unconditional support meant more than she could tell them—though she'd tried more than once.

"Earth to Fallon." The younger woman giggled as she handed Fallon her sweater and purse. *When had she left the room? Damn, I'm really out of it lately.* Walking out the front door, she stood on the top step, trying to remember what vehicle they'd told her to look for.

"It's still hard to believe I have two husbands."

"No wonder you look like you're about to keel over,

honey." The elderly woman walking past winked at Fallon and grinned. Fallon returned the woman's smile then realized she'd already walked out of the building. *Good grief, Fallon. Get your shit together.* Rubbing her hand over her stomach, Fallon wondered what she'd eaten that didn't agree with her. She made a mental note to take an antacid as soon as she got home.

SILAS SHOOK HIS head, wondering how long their wife was going to stand on the step, looking like she was wanted nothing more than to curl up on one of the nearby concrete benches and take a nap. Turning his attention to the man sitting on the other side of the truck, Silas smiled to himself because it appeared Carson was thinking the same thing.

"I can't believe she hasn't figured it out. She's a pharmacist, for fuck's sake." Carson shook his head as he reached for the door handle.

"This is an orthopedic medical complex specializing in pediatric patients. I don't think this situation is in their wheelhouse." Silas knew his explanation was lame but couldn't resist the opportunity to annoy his friend with what Carson referred to as word salad.

"Whatever. Let's go get her before she turns another shade of green. Somebody's bound to call security sooner or later. Damn, she looks completely beat." Carson was out of the truck before Silas could respond. Walking toward Fallon, Silas looked at his watch and smiled.

"We have time to get a quick bite to eat before her appointment." They'd scheduled an after-hours visit to her regular physician when it became clear she hadn't noticed

her body's recent changes. Their hardworking sub attribut-
ed her fatigue to the long hours she was working and her
persistent nausea to something she'd eaten.

Silas smiled as a sense of relief moved over her face
when she saw them walking up the stone stairs. "Thanks
for coming to rescue me. I'm sorry, I forgot if you were
coming in a car or truck. I swear my brain seems to shut
down earlier and earlier." Both men gave her a quick kiss
before leading her back toward the truck. "Do you have
any antacids? I need to start writing down what I eat so I
can figure out what the heck is upsetting my stomach."

"I picked some up on the way here. There's also a bottle of ginger ale, which should help settle your stomach
before your appointment." Carson's comment made her
stop so suddenly her small hand slipped from theirs.

"What appointment? Did I forget an appointment?
Damn, what's wrong with me?" Silas and Carson smiled at
each other over her head. *Not a damned thing a few more
months won't cure.*

"Let's see what the doctor has to say, Chef." Fallon
chewed on her bottom lip, clearly worried something was
seriously wrong. Silas knew she was still weighing her
options when it came to establishing contact with her
parents. Seeing the pain in her eyes whenever the subject
came up was almost more than Silas or Carson could stand.
If they were right and she was pregnant, Fallon didn't need
the added stress of worrying about her family.

As soon as she'd settled into the truck, Fallon swallowed the antacids and leaned her head back. Her eyes
drifted closed. Fallon's breathing evened out before they'd
turned out of the parking lot, and Silas could only shake his
head and grin. When they'd suggested picking up some-

thing to eat, she'd groaned and turned an unattractive shade of green.

An hour later, Silas and Carson were beaming with pride as Fallon stared at the doctor in stunned disbelief. "Pregnant? How? Are you sure?" The elderly man chuckled.

"The *how* question can probably be answered by those two grinning fellows sitting on either side of you. And, yes, I'm sure. I'll have my nurse make you another appointment in a few days. We'll let the shock wear off a bit before we dole out instructions and advice."

The three of them walked out of the office, each speaking at the same time.

"Damn, this is amazing."

"Best day ever."

"Oh my God, I'm pregnant."

The End

Books by Avery Gale

Spellbound
Spellbound – The Knights of Aradia

The Adlers
Brooklyn
London
Austin
Paris
Cleveland
Asia
Kensington
Israel
Bronx
Catalina

The ShadowDance Club
Katarina's Return – Book One
Jenna's Submission – Book Two
Rissa's Recovery – Book Three
Trace & Tori – Book Four
Reborn as Bree – Book Five
Red Clouds Dancing – Book Six
Perfect Picture – Book Seven

Club Isola
Capturing Callie – Book One
Healing Holly – Book Two
Claiming Abby – Book Three

Masters of the Prairie Winds Club
Out of the Storm
Saving Grace
Jen's Journey
Bound Treasure
Punishing for Pleasure
Accidental Trifecta
Missionary Position
Another Second Chance
Star-Crossed Miracles
Dusted Star
Lilly's Choice
Falling for Fallon

The Wolf Pack Series
Mated – Book One
Fated Magic – Book Two
Tempted by Darkness – Book Three

The Knights of the Boardroom
Book One
Book Two
Book Three

The Morgan Brothers of Montana
Coral Hearts – Book One
Dancing with Deception – Book Two
Caged Songbird – Book Three
Game On – Book Four
Well Bred – Book Five

Mountain Mastery
Well Written
Savannah's Sentinel
Sheltering Reagan

The Christmas Painting
Taking Out the Mother of the Bride

I would love to hear from you!

Email:
avery.gale@ymail.com

Website:
www.averygale.com

Facebook:
facebook.com/avery.gale.3

Twitter:
@avery_gale